T5-AFT-505

BAJA

OTHER WORK BY JOHNNY PAYNE

Fiction

Chalk Lake:
A Novel

Kentuckiana

The Ambassador's Son
A Novella

Nonfiction

Voice & Style
The Elements of Fiction Writing Series

Conquest of the New Word:
Experimental Fiction & Translation in the Americas

Drama

The Devil in Disputanta
A Musical Play in Two Acts

BAJA

by

Johnny Payne

Limited Editions Press
Lubbock, Texas
1998

Copyright ©1998 by Johnny Payne

All rights reserved. No part of this book may be reproduced by any means or in any form without written permission from the publisher, except for brief quotations embodied in literary articles or reviews. For information, please address:

Limited Editions Press
2003 16th Street
Lubbock, TX 79401-4609

All characters and geographical settings in this book are fictitious, and any resemblance to actual locales or to any persons, living or dead, is purely coincidental.

Library of Congress Cataloging-in-Publication Data

Payne, Johnny, 1958-
    Baja / by Johnny Payne.
       p.   cm.
    ISBN)-9647515-8-5 (paperback)
    I. Title.
PS3566.A9375B35 1998
813'.54—dc21
                            98-27435
                               CIP

ISBN 0-9647515-8-5

Printed in the United States of America

The Great Salt Lake had kept Vic restless. He'd been turned away from the overfull campground on the fringe of the airport, and was too conspicuously wild-eyed from the packages of No-Doz leftover from his exams to keep driving across the salt flats into Nevada. The state line no doubt teemed with police, who right away would spot his expired license tags. True, they'd expired only three days ago, but all the more reason. Your chances of being caught went down inverse to the amount of time you drove around flouting the law of probability. So he finally parked in gravel on a state beach by the lake. No visible signs forbade him to rest there for a few hours. Curled knees to chest in the back of the station wagon, he ground his teeth. The cold pungency of salt wafted from the lake into his nostrils, giving him a fitful self-image as a fetus preserved in saline for the scrutiny of posterity, set on a mantelpiece in a glass jug as proof that he had never reached fully human proportions.

He sweated, convinced despite all his mumbled denials that the suffocating salt sprang from his own pores, forming a rime on his skin. Only the blue flicker of buoy lights reassured him that the lake was still there. Cannon or sonic booms crackled at intervals, or a thunderstorm gathering in the Rockies behind him to the east. At daybreak, he returned to his normal self: the ex-law student and ex-medical student, chronically deprived of sleep, on edge in the expected ways. The lake spread, steel gray and without froth, quietly submerging its spiral jetty inch by inch. Coffee steam in his nostrils forced an involuntary horsey sigh.

Vic wasn't meant to practice law, that much he'd concluded, but the job at the corporate firm in New York City would at least have helped him pay off the thousands of dollars worth of parking tickets and library fines, compounded by a string of fruitless extensions, that he'd accrued, along with tow bills, service charges on bounced checks, late registration fees to the bursar, the unreturned books that arrived without fail every month from the various book clubs he'd joined at no obligation, the forfeited cleaning deposits on apartments, the credit card overcharges, the emergency loans to pay off other loans, the lien on the classic Packard he'd gone in on with two college roommates, and had to abandon in a long-term parking garage at the airport which he'd used by mistake as short-term parking to pick up a friend. When he misplaced the ticket, the attendant had charged him the maximum, one hundred fifty dollars. First Vic tried to explain to the attendant that he didn't begrudge the airport or its employees the money, but simply didn't have it to give. He and the friend had tried to crash the deceptively sturdy barrier without success. Finally, Vic and the friend threw the Packard into reverse and parked it at an angle in a remote corner of the lot. They began to trot along the aisles, ducking behind parked cars and changing directions often, negotiating stairwells. They were tailed through the maze by airport security in the shape of a turbanned, orthodox-looking enforcer with an earring. Like a surly djinn in a bottle awakened from centuries of hibernation, he glowered from behind the wheel of a Cushman cart much too small to contain him. Somehow they'd managed to escape and take a bus home, but the Packard remained, its wide body taking up two parking spaces emblazoned in fresh canary yellow paint with the legend: *Economy Car Only.*

Most recently, Vic's cartons of books, clothing, and bicycle had been impounded by the attorney slash owner of an eight by four self-storage unit, one of many cubicles forming an inner-city mausoleum for possessions. The contract for it actually referred to the monthly fee as "rent." *Rent shall fall due and payable on the first day of each month. Lessee further agrees that said premises shall not be used as a dwelling, nor shall they be sub-leased for that purpose nor any other, express or implied, not explicitly granted by the terms and stipulations of this covenant. Yea, though I walk through the shadow of Death Valley, I shall fear no evil. Surely goodness and mercy shall follow me all the days of my life, and I shall dwell in the house of the Lord forever. Witnessed this day of _, in the Year of Our Lord, 19_.*

After the campus police had given him two warnings about sleeping in his car on campus property, Vic had slept in the rental storage space for a few nights, in violation of the contract, entombed in the dark recess like a pharaoh with his earthly treasures, lampshades protruding from boxes along with battered editions of hematology texts and books on torts. So, he'd gotten his money's worth. He didn't have anywhere else to house the boxes anyway, even if he could have redeemed them from storage, unless he prevailed yet again upon the few steadfast friends still willing to put up with the chronic poverty of a poor little rich boy. More reprehensible than a life given over to crime was one given over to misdemeanor.

Even his sister Priscilla in Boston, the conspicuously successful broker, who used to refer to Vic affectionately as the "high-risk sibling," refused to loan him one red cent toward the storage bill. She wouldn't accept collect phone calls either, not even when he managed to shout a few illegal (unpaid-for) words of persuasion past the mediating voice of the operator. The operator, he had to say in her favor, had taken his part for an instant before consigning him to the dial tone. *The party appears to be in a state of distress. Are you sure you won't accept the charges?* As for his parents, now living abroad, they reminded him through telephone static as choppy as Pacific waves of the reasonable bargain they had struck: they would send him to Yale for a bachelor's degree, and he would see to the rest. They had done their part.

A yellow notice with an adhesive edge had been attached to the windshield of the station wagon during Vic's futile attempt at sleep. No flashlights had shone in his face in the dead of night, like the pen-light beams of the student rounds he would have made as a medical intern, had he gotten that far, searching out the aftermath of a massive stroke. The cops of Salt Lake City had used polite stealth instead. He could appeal his case at the city courthouse, between the hours of ten and twelve a week from Wednesday, or freely and of his own accord admit guilt immediately upon receipt of this notice and mail his check or money order in the attached, pre-printed envelope. *Do Not Send Cash*.

With a skittering of gravel, Vic returned the car to the road and picked up speed, banishing the gargantuan lake to its proper place as flying scenery. Buttes and cyclone fences hurtled past, then a rest stop without facilities except a broken stone fountain choked with twigs. On the shoulder was a roadside chassis as porous and salty as driftwood. Road hypnosis promised an early onset today as the No-Doz thinned out in his bloodstream. Signpost enticements to distant state parks came and went. He saw a sign in white against a green background, bright as an illuminated manuscript, its reflectors glinting in the daylight. DO NOT GIVE RIDES TO HITCHHIKERS. FEDERAL PENITENTIARY AREA.

Beyond the buttress of an overpass, a figure waited, not lurking, seated atop an oilcloth duffel bag. Vic pulled the car onto the shoulder and idled.

With nothing to counterweight his bag of possessions, the hitchhiker loped, stopping to squint at the telltale dents of the station wagon from a few feet away. When Vic stepped onto the shimmering pavement to open the wagon's gate, the man swung the duffel bag into it with a flourish full of bravado, a sailor in a Gilbert and Sullivan operetta heeding the call of anchors aweigh and dames at sea.

"Your license plate's expired," said the man as soon as he settled into his seat. "Do you want radar? I have a radar gun in my bag that I found in a dumpster in Southern California. With radar, you can figure out the speed of other cars relative to you. You were doing eighty-six when you passed me."

"Sure, climb back there and fetch it. The speedometer's broken." The duffel bag, deteriorating and covered with clayey smears, looked as though it had recently been dug up from some burial ground or other.

"With fifteen miles plus or minus margin for error. So, it could have been seventy-one or a hundred and one." Settling back into his seat, the hitchhiker laid the cylinder across his knees, riding shotgun.

"Let's call it a hundred and one if we don't get stopped," said Vic, "and seventy-one if we do."

The passenger remained silent, moving only his fingers, which stuck out of cycling gloves, like a Chinese mathematician doing rapid calculations. Or maybe he had arthritis. After a long pause he looked at Vic and said, "Did you and I go to high school together?"

Vic returned his gaze. The passenger had dirt embedded in his skin, the stale odor of old sweat, and a face, not unhandsome, seamed by years of private contortions, or maybe just too much sun and too little ozone. There had been that stock market crash a few years ago, when all the commodity traders except Priscilla lost a bundle, and the trust funds of some of his prep school friends had depleted to a fraction of their former worth in a few days. "I don't know. I went to Andover. Did you?"

"Is that near Atlantic City?"

"Close. Close enough. There are some apples there in the back seat I bought at a roadside stand a couple of days ago. I don't know if they're any good. I keep forgetting to eat and drink."

They crunched on Jonathans together, in silence, letting the juice flow. The man ate his down to the seeds.

"You don't know how glad I am to have some company. This road trip is starting to make me weird." He let go of the steering wheel and gave the man's hand a couple of enthusiastic pumps with his sticky fingers. "My name's Vic. Where are you headed?"

"Nevada, possibly. But only for a day or two. I had a good thing going in Atlantic City, buying unused vouchers from the coupon books of losers on the floor of the casinos, and reselling them to winners still in the game. The casino owners didn't mind, because it meant more dollars circulating. It's not like Nevada. I mean they personally care about your fortunes in Atlantic City."

"Give me a break. Casino owners don't care whether you live or die."

"I'm telling the truth. I feel bad for Donald Trump right now, all his financial troubles."

"You feel sorry for Donald Trump?" With one hand Vic smoothed back his flaring hair, alive in the warm airstream of the open window, to entertain this new thought. "If I had his checkbook for one day, I could pay off all my loans. If I could cure one of the big diseases—or even a small one—there are so many. I spent summer before last working in a lab for one of the most prestigious doctors at a school back East. They're paying him a fortune to do leukemia research, and he's like a corporation. He's in no hurry, believe you me. I tried to develop a cure myself. I stayed after hours reading the research, but at that rate, it would have taken me two hundred years."

"Well, Donald Trump means well. Setting reasonable odds, he gives a tithe back to the gamblers. You don't find his croupiers laying a heavy hand on the roulette wheel, making the silver ball jump where they want it to go. I've seen plenty of that in Nevada, and I know. Before I went to Atlantic City, I was living in an abandoned gas station in Manhattan, Lower East side, until the cop show of a certain famous television actor, whose name I won't mention for fear of a libel suit, got cancelled after the pilot episodes. He took over the gas station, evicted all the tenants, and used it to sell Christmas trees. Called it Yule Buy Trees. Subliminal, see? So when I happened into the coupon business in Atlantic City, I felt flush. Whatever his ex-wife may tell you, I consider Donald Trump the patron saint of the homeless. Living in the parking lots of his casinos, we brokers kept our overhead low. A few commuted every day from Delaware, where they slept on the beaches. With the food and drink coupons, you could eat prime rib, have a cocktail or two after work. An honest living. But inside of a year, we got way too many coupon traders on the floor, some of them conning winners out of their bonus coupons. It set the wrong moral tone, a few tourists complained, and our livelihood dried up. Now, I don't know where I'm headed. I might have to stop in Vegas for a while, as much as I hate it."

Vic edged the station wagon into the right lane, following the path marked out by the sloping line of traffic cones, some of them knocked over on their sides. In the left lane, bulldozers and men in orange mesh vests with jackhammers were destroying the pavement, sending plumes of chalky, pulverized grit into the air. "To tell you the truth, I don't know where I'm headed either. I wish I could find a place in the desert and be done with driving. I drove all the way to New York from San Francisco, because I'm supposed to show up for a job that begins tomorrow morning. Sixty-one thousand bucks a year to start, and that's just until I pass my bar exam. Because of my medical background, they're going to put me to work right off doing research on a case where one big company is suing another one for trademark infringement over some plastic disposable syringe that they both manufacture. It's the same type of syringe that kept washing up on the Jersey shores all last summer, so I'm not sure why they're both so eager to claim it. On the turnpike I actually started to shake. At first I thought it was the car, because the wheels are out of alignment and it shudders between about fifty and sixty miles an hour. Then I realized it was me. So I gassed up and headed straight back."

"Sixty-one thou? You're a chump. Do you know what I could do with sixty-one thousand dollars?"

"Blow it at the casino tables."

"Yeah, you're probably right." The traffic cones ended as suddenly as they had appeared. As the station wagon pulled alongside a van cruising in the passing lane, its driver talking on a car phone, the hitchhiker took aim across Vic at the van's passenger window. The driver applied his brakes suddenly, dropped the phone, and his van veered, weaved, and fell back. "I couldn't get a bead on him. Anyway, I know how you feel. I had a great job working at an adult book store. Good pay, and you really got to study a cross-section of humanity. They had peep shows in the back, with nude dancers, and on lunch break I'd stick my eye to the hole for a few minutes.

The dancer fiddled with herself, and I kind of dug watching that. But some of the customers would stick their tongues through the holes and have her shimmy over and rub against them. Disgusting. Very poor hygiene. One afternoon, I was ringing up a rental, like always, and I realized that all the women on the video cartons were looking at me from the shelves, their heads thrown back, their mouths open, their eyes accusing me. I knew that I was the blackest of sinners. I had to go live out in the desert, like Saint Jerome. I hitched back West and lived in a rusted-out car in the bottom of a little gully, where I raised the leafiest cannabis plants you ever saw, in the engine cavity, using a rich mixture of cow dung and soil. I was pretty methodical about it. You have a girl friend?"

Vic clicked on the radio and gave the hitchhiker a hard look, meaning to chasten him for introducing the subject of Vic's love life in that sordid context. But the No-Doz had dried up; he was crashing fast. The familiar scent of the worn rawhide coiled about the steering wheel absurdly pierced through the stronger odor of the hitchhiker, making Vic's knees go weak. A slow ballad about dreams, sung by the Cowboy Junkies, came in sweet and crystalline. "She's teaching classical literature at a prep school in California called the Horace Academy. This is her car that we're driving in." Technically, she'd given the car to Vic, instructing him to change the registration into his name, saying that she didn't want any of his upcoming accidents on her head. She didn't consider the car dependable enough to have on the Southern California freeways, and so had left it with him for his cross-country drive.

"Hm. Sounds like maybe there's heartbreak involved. She dump you?"

"No."

"You dump her?"

"Let's change the topic."

"Okay, okay. I guess she couldn't have dumped you, otherwise you wouldn't be driving her wheels. But listen, I understand. You're on the cusp of a brilliant career in trademark negotiation, and still your heart aches, and you're not sure exactly why. Take as a case in point the work I've been doing over the past few years. I was trained as a physicist. I didn't stay in the profession, because of a conspiracy against me among my scientific brethren, but I've been conducting experiments on my own all the same, like you, without any outside support. I sent some of my findings to one of the big laboratories, because they have grants where they'll buy ideas from independent thinkers and refine them in their own labs. Here's the thing: I've discovered the smallest physical particle known to man—I call it the Space Particle. It's smaller than a quark, smaller than a Z, any of those. Those look like boulders next to this. And after having the chance to study my proposal for free, gratis, those bastards turn me down for a grant. I know they're going to use my data somewhere down the road. But I'm not going to let myself get agitated over the question of rights. If the scientific community wants to award me the Nobel Prize, fine. If not, then forget about it. I'm going back into the wilderness. I've steadily been building a space ship between jobs, for years, out in the desert close to where I lived in that car hull. Nobody but me knows the exact spot. With the sophisticated technology they got, the Soviets could be photographing your license plate right this second, and seeing that your registration has expired. But this place they wouldn't be able to locate. All I can say is it's underneath a kiva, a real one, and only I know about it. A little piece of land I came into. One day I was on it, looking for a cool place to get away from the sun, because it's very hot there, and underneath some dilapidated ruins on the property, I found a burial chamber. I'd crawled into a little cavern for shade, and saw some natural fissures in the basalt, so I squeezed through, taking a flashlight with me, and there they were. Catacombs, all sealed up so nobody from the outside would discover them. Hundreds of graves with the bones laid out under stone cairns, or in wall niches and stone cribs. I haven't told anybody about it but you, because it's a sacred burial spot, and nobody should disturb it. But right then and there I knew I had to start constructing my space ship inside that place, where it would remain hidden from view. When I'm done building, the ship is going to be powered by the Space Particle. The particle is similar to heavy water, only much much smaller, and do you know how I'm going to live in space? Do you?"

Vic stared ahead through the windshield, not meeting the hitchhiker's piercing eye. There certainly weren't many rest stops along this road. "Uh, no. I couldn't really venture a guess."

"Off the by-products. I'm going to live off the by-products of the Space Particle, because it will produce water to drink and oxygen to breathe. And I'm going to be the only survivor, because Armageddon is at hand. A sudden downturn in the real estate market. Houses will be built but not dwelt in. The water table's sinking, the underground river is running dry. Think about it. You see those salt flats out there? They are chock full of missile silos. Everywhere you look, everywhere you can't see, missile silos are waiting, Vic. That's the reason for the sadness you can't put your finger on."

Vic nodded, trying to look properly pensive and respectful as the hitchhiker continued, with increasing heat, to expound on his theories. In case the guy really was a prophet, he didn't want to cross him. Saint Jerome had probably sounded much like this in 400 A.D. to travelers riding past him on their donkeys. And even if the man wasn't a prophet, Vic wished to avoid doing anything that might provoke his passenger into cracking him upside the head with the radar gun. The man finally lapsed into another silence, with his look of a Chinese mathematician, his fingers protruding from the bicycle gloves and interlocked around the gun.

They rode that way for a while, neither of them speaking, until a cluster of buildings at last appeared ahead of them. "I need to make a stop at a place up here that's a diner and automobile museum," said the hitchhiker. "I hope you don't mind."

Vic quickly agreed. "Oh, not at all. Would you like to stop for lunch? I'm buying. I'm finally starting to get hungry and thirsty. I don't think I've peed once today or yesterday." He had about two hundred dollars left, after having spent three hundred or so the day before for a new radiator and some replacement hoses, and decided he could afford to spring for the meal. This way he would at least have a chance to get the guy out of the car, and afterward he could give him a lift further down the road or not, depending on how the conversation progressed over lunch. He knew what Andrea would say, but he hadn't made up his mind definitely one way or the other.

It had always irked Andrea that Vic had a way of becoming involved in conversations with people like this. If somebody came to the door brandishing a copy of *Watchtower*, Vic couldn't resist inviting the person in. Or, she would say, "When we go for a romantic afternoon to relax on the beach at San Gregorio, and all I want is to snuggle in your beautiful golden chest hair, do acrobatics in the coastal wind with our cloth kite, and try out my new tanga, then some elephant seal, some naked swarthy coot living on the nudist part of the beach in a driftwood shack always ambles down, gloms onto you and starts discussing theosophy in excruciating detail. They can smell you out a mile away. Am I starting to get cellulite? Is that why I can't hold your attention?"

Vic's friends in law school had lusted discreetly after blonde and supple Andrea. They often reminded him how lucky he'd been to find a hardnosed classics major who looked like the cosmopolitan sister of a surfer chick. The Latin Lover, they called her. Not long after she and he had started to date, she suffered a serious accident on a motor scooter, when she neglected to wear a helmet because it would mess up her hair. The concussion kept her in the hospital for a couple of weeks, flirting with death while she held on for dear life to the hand of Vic, a boyfriend she'd barely gotten a chance to know, and begged him not to leave her side.

While he devoted himself to pouring her glasses of tepid water from the octagonal styrofoam pitcher at her bedside, he missed his moot court performance, after putting in weeks of solid preparation for once in his life. He'd had to endure the scorn of a retired Federal Appeals Court Justice. Thanks to that single absence, Vic had blown whatever slim chance he'd built up for a federal clerkship. "I'm not keeping you from anything, am I?" Andrea would ask fretfully in her lucid moments.

"No," Vic would say, "I've got my tomes right here," and produce one of his thicker textbooks from her bedside table for inspection, to put her at her ease. After the hospital released Andrea, she wanted to move in with Vic right away, an arrangement which he consented to, but at times her passionate affection for him had struck him more as imprinting than love. He'd simply been there when she opened her eyes.

The plastic surgery on her face, performed seamlessly by a colleague of her father's, left scarcely a scar unless you looked very hard for it. But she worried about her appearance, always asking Vic how she looked, and started to obsess about her weight. Andrea started running ungodly distances in the foothills. Since the important work in law school, by its nature, could best be accomplished by doing nothing then going on a fanatical, sleepless binge the last week of the semester, Vic often kept her company. Running the Dish, everybody around there called it.

At the highest point in the foothills, with views of the Marin headlands when the fog burned off, the path wound around a huge, powerful satellite dish, fenced off with high voltage wire and supposedly used by NASA to gather information about weather and who knew what other distant radio signals. During the Northern California spring, when tough, clovery ground cover sprouted, the university leased the foothills to local ranchers to graze their cattle. The drought had been on for several years straight, with record low water marks in reservoirs at a time of record increases in livestock breeding. With water rationing in effect and water subsidies discontinued, the ranchers were taking their pastureland where they could get it. The running paths were punctuated throughout with iron cattle guards, and as Vic and Andrea jogged together, taking care to hit the metal bars just right so as not to turn their ankles, the cows did their desultory cropping, sometimes jutting their rear-ends out onto the cracked pavement, or else knelt together just off the paths, placidly eyeing the few runners hardy enough to brave the scorching midday heat.

"That one has a dreamy expression a lot like yours," said Andrea, taking a cattle guard in two perfect strides. "Do you suppose he's ruminating on the Apocrypha?" She teased Vic that she'd fallen for him precisely because he seemed oblivious to his Byronic good looks, as she called them. "Women are practically killing themselves in the law school, Vic, trying to meet you, and you want to tell them about the Kabbala. They've finally figured out who Magic Johnson is, and you throw Gershom Scholem at them. It drives them crazy. And that's all you better talk with them about," she continued back at the cottage, in that habit she had of completing a thought hours, days, or weeks after she started it, snaking over top of him on the mattress, her running shorts like a silky skin about to be shed.

She had finished her degree a semester early, and didn't know what to do with herself besides prepare elaborate rice tables with seven kinds of chutney, without eating much of it herself, and work as a Greek and Latin tutor to sulking teenage boys whose humiliation was made complete by their being bested in a dead language by a sharp-looking babe. Sometimes, while washing dishes, he listened through the screen door to her, at the glass-topped patio table with one of her students, beneath the dwarf lemon tree, as she worked effortlessly through noun declensions the way a seasoned musician might play through a familiar fugue. With a self-dismissive flick of her tapered tennis wrist, Andrea batted off Vic's praise, claiming that she was in hiatus from intellectual life, and going through her spandex glamour girl phase. Vic countered that he knew better, that what

11

she was really doing was preparing to inherit the earth. And she planned for him to inherit it with her.

She did everything well. He had nothing to complain of. On their winter camping trips to the volcanic back-country of Mount Lassen, she roughed it without complaint, carrying her thirty pounds of gear with élan—a word that didn't seem to fit with camping except in reference to her—as they climbed in meditative silence among the billows of steam roiling up from under the drifts of snow, where hot springs lay beneath petrified magma. She loved his mongrel dog Gorby, a hairy creature given to weaseling his way into silt-coated storm drains. She permitted the dog to nuzzle her with slack black lips and to shed copiously in the plush back seat of her parents' borrowed car, even though she was allergic to dog hair and had to keep taking out her extended-wear contact lenses to squirt them with solution.

Vic's only real hypocrisy in their relationship had been his using the pretext of his upcoming job in Manhattan, the one he now wasn't going to show up at, to stymie their romance. Andrea would have loved nothing better than to move to New York with him. Though she harbored fantasies of eventual marriage and a baby, she made a point of never mentioning either, except once when they had drunk too much bad ouzo on top of greasy souvlaki, and she said the only time she ever wanted to be that sick again was if she was carrying his child. Far from trying to mold him to suit her taste, she was amenable to every possibility. If he wanted to chase his idealism and do public service law, that was something she could believe in as well. He simply had to say the word. If he opted for corporate law, there were always weekends for pro-bono. The legal profession was even some-thing she might participate in. She had taken the LSAT, and scored high, to show him she was capable of succeeding in a professional career, if push came to shove.

Couldn't he see that she simply wanted to be with him, that she was insanely in love with him, but that didn't mean she would become some kind of passive burden if they moved to New York together? She always found projects of her own to keep herself occupied, didn't she? What did he want of her? She was twenty-two years old, for Christ's sake. He had no idea how difficult it was, with all the screwed-up, mixed-up, contradictory advice that he and her parents and sisters and the rest of the universe kept laying on her, and her being self-aware and rational and Phi Beta Kappa about it hadn't really helped a whole hell of a lot. He sure didn't seem to mind fucking her brains out even after they had been fighting, and she suspected that a little tussle beforehand, like that time he actually threw her down on the bed, even turned him on a bit. A little rutting was never amiss, right?

But why did he insist on humiliating her by pulling away from her innocent caresses and complaining that she was clinging to him too hard? Didn't he realize that guys were hitting on her all the time, she didn't mean those moony-eyed students of hers, but real grown-up guys, hunks with brains, like when she worked as a temp secretary for that film development company, men were pressuring her all the time to go out, but she always told them about Vic, that she had to get home, realizing of course that he would not in fact be home, but instead out auditing some fatuous evening seminar on numerology and the Russian Futurists, and to get these aspiring actors and nouveau playboys off her back she had to go so far as to concoct a story about how she was engaged, and wear a little jewel ring she'd bought downtown at a pawn shop and kept in her purse, the oldest trick in the book, just to get some respite, knowing all the while that Vic would have been furious had he discovered that she was spreading a rumor about their moving in the direction of marriage, however slowly.

He had not, in fact, gotten furious. She had—furious like a Fury. In that same week, he lost his wallet, containing his ID cards, the two credit cards that hadn't yet been cancelled, and a month's wages as a research assistant, paid in cash instead of check at his request of course. He'd laid his wallet and drink in the grass next to the outdoor cinder track behind the stadium while he ran a few laps and, not surprisingly, the wallet wasn't there when he went to retrieve it. They couldn't make rent, and decided to move to a short-term sublet, since money in hand was suddenly getting tight. Andrea was used to getting every penny of her deposit back, even on utilities and soft-drink bottles. She added up the groceries in her head faster than the checker could scan them, and the humiliation of the experience of finding herself in arrears for the first time ever didn't sit well with her. Vic had already screwed up his credit record for life, no matter what amends he might try to make later on, and if he thought he was going to do the same to hers so early on, he'd better think again. He was as bad off as one of those people whose lives are ruined by the monetary excesses of somebody with the exact same legal name, causing them to be hounded unjustly to the ends of the earth by collection agencies. Or actually he would be the one to destroy the life of some other poor innocent working stiff with the same name, he himself was the doppelgänger.

Then, on the day of their move, after she was teary-eyed from wiping the baseboards with ammonia and having countless five-minute spats with him and making love twice on the bare mattress in the nearly empty cottage, with the sheets already stripped off and the frame loaded in the borrowed pickup truck and two glasses of warm ale sitting on the carpet, to top it all off he then lost his dog Gorby, by letting him wander around without a leash at the new place, which lay right across the creek from one corner of the foothills. They'd left him cooped up in the truck cab whimpering and trying to force his muzzle through the crack in the window while they argued. When they let him out and scrambled across the dry creek bed onto the university lands so the dog could romp a little, he sniffed and peed to stake out his new personal territory, racing from bush to bush in an orbit so wide that Vic, laughing, rubbed the pooch's belly and asked him if he was trying to mark off the boundaries of the Lousiana Purchase with his urine. "His master's dog," said Andrea with a sob in her throat. At sunset, Vic had left him to guard the new digs while he and she went back for a final load, and when they returned, the dog had disappeared.

Already exhausted, their nerves twangy, they then had to spend all night looking for Gorby, scrutinizing every shadowy bush the headlights fell across, for shapes as sharp-edged and illusory as finger-animals in front of a slide projector, their cries echoing off the dark mounds of the foothills as they waved their flashlights like semaphores. The hulking silhouettes of sleeping cattle started up and crashed away. They never did find the dog, then or later. He and Andrea were afraid that Gorby had caught his leg in one of the cattle guards in the dark, perhaps broken it. Vic also had the idea that the satellite dish might be putting out a high-pitched frequency, and that seeking out the noise, the dog had clambered to the crest and bounded into the high voltage fence.

The loss of his dog distressed Vic far more than the loss of his wallet had. He began to talk nonstop, trying to console them both, speculating that maybe Gorby would join up with some wild dogs, he knew there were untold numbers of stray cats living underneath the law school, he'd heard them meowing in the heating ducts. He often set out food for them, pieces of bologna or french fries, and skunks were always coming down out of the foothills, looking for water and garbage, so there had to be packs of wild dogs as well. He just hoped Gorby would learn to adapt and wouldn't get attacked by them as an outsider because of the different smell of his coat.

"What in God's name are you raving about?" she shouted. "I hope you realize that nobody else but me would have put up with your bullshit for this long. Why are you so intent on self-destructing? Is our relationship too perfect for you? Does my happy childhood bother you? Does it go against your epic sensibility? My parents' divorce should count for something, anyway. And my accident, even if it was just on a motor scooter. I hate to tell you this, you stupid teen heartthrob, but Ajax is a certified lunatic, and the slaughtered goats and sheep are long since buried in the earth. So you might as well stop lamenting them."

But he knew that for all her Athenian wrath, she would be willing to tolerate the many lapses he'd committed and more if he would ask her to live in New York with him. Andrea believed in her heart that once he started to work a regular job, he would put away childish things and cleave unto his wife. He would get out of debt and the passion would remain between them till death did them part, with the help of electoral campaigns every two years, and an occasional new piece of lingerie. She remained convinced to the end that he was being deliberately perverse when he did things like losing his wallet. It was simply a case of prolonged adolescence, a charming enough trait in a man as long as he learned to channel it into TV sports.

She unpacked all of her possessions into the new place, and began right away to arrange their spices in the rack, the different blends of curry by gradations of color, to carve out a space for the two of them to start afresh. She could get a short-term loan from the credit union, or, in a pinch, from one or the other of her parents, to cover for his lost wages. He left his possessions boxed up, and mentally gave up the ones they held in common, as well as those that remained even slightly in doubt. Self-knowledge wasn't his forte, but he knew enough to foresee that their cohabitation in Manhattan would have started as a disaster, and ended as something worse. Even so, they still slept together most nights in their sublet, until she announced one morning that she had secured a job teaching at the Horace Academy, and would fly down there within a few days.

The billboard in the arid expanse of field beyond the parking lot of the restaurant announced 4, 319, 675, 802 People Have Never Been to Oasis, Nevada. Right away Vic noticed that the numerical figure on the billboard included each of the ten digits once, without repetition. A television satellite dish crowned a low rectangular prefab building named The Mirage. Its windows were all plugged by leaky air conditioning units. A sign in the window said that The Mirage served sweet and sour burritos, gyros, breakfast twenty-four hours a day, and offered slot machines, blackjack, roulette, and pai-gow poker. It was eleven o'clock in the morning, and a van and two other cars were parked in the lot. The van, which they had parked next to, looked vaguely familiar to Vic. He'd probably seen it on the road. There weren't too many vehicles on this stretch of highway, or too many places to eat, for that matter, so it was only natural that you'd keep seeing the same vehicles, the same people.

"Is this where you wanted to stop?"

"Yeah, I thought you might enjoy playing a few hands of blackjack after we eat. I'll watch. The great thing is, anywhere you go in Nevada you can gamble, even the most solitary outpost. Vegas is just bigger."

It felt good to exercise his stiff limbs by walking about while the car's metal hood made crinkling sounds. He'd been gripping the steering wheel so hard his knuckles were sore. He broke into a trot, scooped up a handful of sandy loose soil from a planter at the edge of the parking lot, and flung it into the air. Granules stuck to his palm. "I wish Andrea was here with us right now," he shouted, wiping his hand on his jeans. He sprinted back over to the station wagon, feeling a lightheaded rush from the sudden movement after sitting so long, and grabbed the hitchhiker's shoulder.

"Okay, tell me what you think of this idea. I've never really gambled, but I'll try what's left of my luck. If I go completely broke, I'll have to take the job as an attorney, right? That would make a lot of people happy. My parents, my sister, Andrea. My creditors, especially. And I'll take you wherever you want to go and then drive back to New York. But if I win enough to pay off all my debts—except my student loans, of course—then you can have this rattletrap car and drop me off at the nearest airport, because I'll buy myself a plane ticket to L.A."

"You'll give me the car?"

"Sure, sure. Word of honor." Vic reached in the passenger side, dug a wad of receipts out of the glove compartment, and started to add them up. "God, I wish Andrea was here," he repeated, uncrumpling one or two of the colored slips of paper. "She'd have this stuff added up in a second. I was saving these to see if I could itemize them on my taxes next year. Obviously, I'd have to talk to an accountant first." He tossed them through the open back window, where they fell in a clump to the floorboard. "I need to win roughly five or six thousand bucks to get out of the hole. It's a question of will. I've been giving it some serious thought these past couple of days, and I think Andrea and I should get back together." He appreciated the care with which she did everything. Even her driving style, so meticulous, which used to annoy him, was something he was starting to miss. Whenever she reached an intersection, she came to a full and complete stop.

Vic remembered sitting in the station wagon at a red light in the Bay Area at three in the morning, back when they were still together. They'd been parked somewhere, necking after a midnight movie, and had decided to go to a certain twenty-four hour donut place, because she was suddenly hungry, and she knew that the glazed donuts there came out of the oven hot at three a.m. or so. There were no other cars at the quiet inter-section, and the red light didn't seem like it was ever going to turn green. He'd tried very hard to persuade her to just run the red light, arguing that the purpose of red lights, of the Platonic red light anyway, was the avoidance of accidents, and since there was absolutely no one in sight at the intersection, even if she ran it she'd still be obeying the law. They'd ended up having a big argument about it, and never did get around to buying the hot glazed donuts, then or later. The fact that she was well-versed in Platonism and the philosophy of the sophists hadn't helped his cause any. The issue had soon become moot, because while they were arguing, the light turned green. They'd sat there at the intersection yelling at one another through several changes of red and green, without coming any closer to resolving the matter, producing stomach acid that might have been assuaged easily enough by a few mouthfuls of glazed donut and a carton of milk. They were lucky nobody had come hurtling along in the night and slammed into them from behind.

"There are so many forgotten towns in this country, especially out here in the Southwest, where she and I could hole up together long enough to forget about all the bad history we've built up between us. If we could do that, and only have each other to deal with, and not all these other pressures, I really think that things could work out for us."

"That sounds very romantic. I haven't been with a woman in nine years. When I quit the porn shop, I took a vow of celibacy. Not that I was getting laid anyway."

"Will they teach me the gambling rules in there?"

"Oh, you'll pick it up," said the hitchhiker. "The rules are the least of it."

While they sat on bar stools soaking in the air conditioning and chewing Oriental burritos wrapped in flour tortillas tough as latex, Vic leafed through the single section of this week's issue of the *Oasis Sentinel*, which had been left lying, badly folded and stained with water rings, on the bar. After much U.S. pressure, a new extradition treaty had just been signed with Mexico, with promises of stricter patrolling at the border, stiffer penalties for drugs, in spite of the fact that the Mexican government's complaint that the problem was on the demand side.

"Listen," said the hitchhiker, producing a grimy, creased envelope from one of his voluminous trouser pockets. "Since you're thinking of heading west, I want you to have this. You're looking for a place to be with this girl and forget about everything else, this might be the ticket."

"What is it?" Vic unfolded the stapled, dogeared sheets of paper inside. It looked like a contract of some kind, one that had been gotten out and read over many times.

This interim deed, when redeemed in person at the designated office of SUNCORP INTERNATIONAL, entitles the bearer to 1.2 acres of real property in the fabulous proposed development MAYAN PARADISE on the incomparably scenic Sea of Cortez, south of Bahia de los Angeles on Mexico's coveted Baja Peninsula. This is not a gimmick! An actual, existing and surveyed lot has already been assigned to this coupon number, at the precise latitude and longitude specified below, and merely needs to be claimed. The deed is fully transferable to heirs and assigns, and may also be redeemed at a cash value of three hundred REALBUK™ dollars, should the holder so desire. Holder relinquishes all subsoil rights to the Mexican government. Once projected development is completed, and sewage, electricity, and access roads are provided, improved property will be reassessed, and holder has option to resell to SUNCORP at original value, or complete purchase at rates to be established by SUNCORP. Monthly maintenance fees will be set at an unspecified future date. SUNCORP assumes no liability for failure to complete projected development. In such an eventuality, property will revert to the Mexican government on Jan. 1, 2019.

"Promotional thing by a pencil company," said the hitchhiker.

"Why are you giving it to me?"

"Let's just say I'm returning the favor. You treated me decent, now I'm treating you decent. You said you're looking for a place in the desert, right? I've never told anybody, but this is where the catacombs are, underneath it."

"But this is your sacred spot. You can't give it to me."

"I'm not going to need it any more in a couple of weeks. As soon as I finish the spaceship, I'll be leaving. You'll notice I haven't even actually claimed the land yet. That's because I ain't going to relinquish my subsoil rights to the Mexican government. The land on top, it's of no interest to me. All I want is the space underneath. So, you just give me a little time to finish my ship, before you claim it, and it's yours."

"Well, maybe I'll go look it over. But if you change your mind, you'll let me know."

"I ain't going to change my mind. Do I look fickle to you?"

"I guess not," said Vic. He went back to reading the contract and pored it over between minute sips of beer. Likely as not, the deed was a developer's scam, one of those places where people ended up sitting forever on an arid tract in the middle of nowhere, waiting for the promised amenities. But that would be perfect. No condos, no beachfront hotels taking over the local economy and driving up the prices of basic necessities, no artificial overnight cities like Cancun materializing in the wilderness out of nowhere, *creatio ex nihilo*, with wide-screen televisions and cable in the bars so the weekend tourists from Southern California wouldn't miss any of the Lakers games. Just desert and sea, harsh and unforgiving. He'd leave it in its pristine state. It would be cheap. He and Andrea could live in the station wagon for a time down in Baja, if need be, until he could set up.

When he looked up, the hitchhiker had disappeared into the adjacent casino room, blocked from sight by a beaded curtain. The ring of the invisible slot machines and the occasional clatter of coins sounded like the staccato report of the pressurized air hose still in Vic's ears. He couldn't shake off the road noise. Masses of air moved across the big sky, pushing cumulus clouds before them like an armada of parade floats, high-pressure and low-pressure systems collided, and his sinus cavities expanded and cracked in the parched air. In the past twenty-four hours, he had crossed the continental divide at least five times without changing directions, driving toward troughs of water as viscous as mercury that evaporated as he neared each one.

Taking the rest of his mug of beer with him, its foam dissipating into constellations of carbonated amber bubbles, Vic pushed through the clack of the beaded curtains in search of the hitchhiker. An old woman with a bandana wrapped around her head sat at one of the slot machines, mumbling imprecations and holding in her lap a cardboard bucket filled with nickels. With the dexterity of a shiva, she was feeding the nickels as fast as she could not only into her machine, but also into the machines on either side of her. The hitchhiker was nowhere in sight, and all the casino tables remained covered with fan-shaped plastic tarps except for one blackjack table that said Three Dollar Minimum. In the seat farthest to the right sat a lone man with the rangy build and downcast, pensive head of a midmorning drunk. He wore a Stetson, photosensitive glasses, an Izod shirt and blue jeans. Next to him on an empty stool lay a cane with a brass horse's head for a knob.

The dealer was a rawboned woman covered with moles and skin tags. On a stool in the semi-dark the sole cocktail waitress loitered, of monolithic face, her thighs splayed and ample, her reclining posture that of a carven fertility goddess in a dry country, the pleats of her mini-dress wadded in her crotch. The dealer bore down on Vic with one leaden brow, silently commanding him to take a seat at her table. He obeyed. Her profusion of skin tags seemed the result of ritual scarification. He worked up a a drop or two of spittle, spat on his chapped hands, and rubbed them together. Vic handed two twenties to the dealer, who shoved the bills with a plastic plunger into an oblong slot in the table, and returned to him a handful of red and white, official-looking embossed chips. Vic fingered the serrated edges. He would start conservatively, for once. After he placed three white chips, the minimum, in the white circle in front of him, then his and the man's cards were dealt face up: a nine and four for the man, a six and three for Vic, and a six showing for the dealer.

"Hit me," said the man, and she did. The card was a jack of clubs. "Shit. The cowboy's runt brother. Busted again. That deck's full of nothing but face cards, except when I need one." He had the tanned, weatherbeaten look of a native Westerner. But Vic also noted the un-accountable moon-face, and a plastic inhaler lying next to the pile of poker chips.

"I suppose I'll take another too," said Vic.

"Please don't bend the cards. This may not be Vegas, but it ain't Sunday night bingo either. Just scrape them toward you if you want a hit."

Vic scraped the felt cloth. She gave him an eight. That made seven-teen.

"I'd hold tight if I was you, and play the odds," said the cowpoke. "Even if you only tie with the dealer, you get your money back." The dealer glowered but didn't speak.

"All right, I'll stick. Thanks." The dealer turned up her down card. It was an ace. "See? Dealer has to take a hit on soft seventeen," the man said.

"Soft seventeen? What's that? It sounds like the year after sweet six-teen."

"The ace swings, as either one or eleven." The next card, thrown atop the dealer's hand, was a seven, followed by a queen of hearts. She raked in the cards, and shoved three matching white chips into Vic's circle. He let them lie.

"Anyone for a drink?" asked the waitress at his elbow, still partially eclipsed in shadow. There were rows of overhead lamps. Her chiaroscuro didn't accord with the laws of physics as he knew them. Maybe she was casting her own shadow. "Give me another beer," the moon-faced man said. Vic rubbed at the dust in his lashes and ordered tequila. The waitress moved toward the bar, throwing behind her a dark stripe no wider than the band of a stone sundial.

"You didn't see a guy with cycling gloves come in here, did you? He was sort of with me." No, the man hadn't noticed anybody come in. He was kind of waiting for somebody himself, but the fellow didn't look like he was going to show after all. By the time the waitress set the cocktail napkin and tequila down next to him, Vic was already twenty or thirty dollars up. He took several gulps of tequila into his mouth, swished it around, and let it slide all at once down his throat. Its afterburn was delicious, leeching the road grit out of his gums. For a few hands he stood pat with anything twelve or over, figuring that with as many face cards as there were in the deck, he'd let the dealer have the chance to bust herself, the way she had the first time. Then for a while he took improbable chances, to see what would happen, asking for a hit even when he had sixteen or seventeen. Either way, he was winning most of his hands. Once in a while, after the deal showed her up card to be an ace, she would ask him if he wanted insurance. He didn't know exactly what the term referred to, but he'd gotten along, ever since he came of legal age, without health, life, or car insurance, so he certainly wasn't about to start taking out insurance on poker hands, and he didn't inquire further.

Vic played unmindful of how many chips he was building up, but he kept steadily increasing his bets. This must be what they meant by playing a streak. Though the dealer had acted surly at the beginning, especially at Vic's bending the cards, she appeared indifferent to her own unlucky run and the chips he was amassing. After a certain number of hands he surmised that her play, unlike his, was bound by a strict set of house rules. She had to take another card if her hand showed sixteen or under, and was required to stand pat if she had seventeen or more. No decisions were asked of her; she simply executed the arbitrary and immutable laws of the game.

After they had played for a considerable stretch, and she'd offered the yellow plastic card to each of them in turn several times, to cut a deck as thick as a helping of strata, she gave a small self-deprecating bow as another dealer in a black bowtie, with the face of a bank manager called over to deal with some bookkeeping irregularity, appeared at her side to replace her. The cowpoke tossed her a five-dollar chip, and Vic did likewise. She took their offerings and retired. "You're looking pretty good over there," he said to Vic. "You must be six or seven hundred dollars up." The man's own pile had visibly diminished. He harumphed a few times, trying without success to bring phlegm out of his chest, and took two hits off his inhaler. "Wish I had your cards. Man, these air inversions in the valley just kill me."

"What exactly is it that ails you?"

"Nothing spectacular. Severe asthma."

"You're taking Albuterol?"

"That and a whole passel of corticosteroids."

A ceiling fan whirred above them, sending down a choppy column of air and white noise. "I wasn't expecting my stack to build so fast. It's pure beginner's luck. I'm not sure how much I've got," said Vic. "I'm working on a dowry. There's a woman in Southern California, a teacher."

"Did you answer an ad in one of those singles magazines? I tell you, I've turned up some losers that way. I haven't quite got the hang of describing myself yet."

"Well, actually, she's somebody I know. I just came into a little stake of land where we might homestead. She doesn't know about it yet, but I'm sure I can sell her on the idea, if I put it the right way. I need enough to get me to the West Coast, and out of debt, and a little nest egg."

"If you're not playing for recreation, you better start easing back on the betting, friend. A run can only last so long. I know what I'm talking about."

"Yeah, but since I'm riding high, I may as well try to double my money, at least. I'm desperate to build up a little cash reserve. I can't show up empty-handed, otherwise she won't take me seriously. See, we were having money problems for a while, and that's part of the reason we split up."

"Don't double up. Now that's just sheer stupidity, if I may say so."

"Why? The way I figure it, I'm as likely to win on a big bet as a small one. The cards don't know the difference. What's going to make me lose is if I psych myself out. The dealer's not really playing against me, and has to stay or go according to a fixed number. Isn't that so?"

"You're right about that, but there are the poker gods to be reckoned with as well. Don't forget about them."

"Let's just say for the sake of argument that you're correct. If the poker gods are controlling my whole future, there's no sense me trying to defy them. You know what happened to Oedipus when he did."

"Friend of yours?"

Vic smiled. His body felt pleasantly numb as he finished emptying another whopping glass of tequila. "According to my girlfriend, yes. Ever heard of hubris? That's my vice. But you and my elusive passenger have got me feeling superstitious, so I'll deliver myself over to the poker gods straight off on this upcoming hand. Double or nothing. I'm only holding back this five-dollar chip so that I don't have to make good on a promise I made about what I'd do if I went completely bust." He deposited it in his shirt pocket. "Just a formality, though, because I plan to win this hand."

The man sat out to watch the play. Vic pushed every one of his chips into the circle, and the hand was dealt. The new dealer gave himself an ace showing, and Vic a king and a seven.

"Tough break," said the cowpoke. "But you might still pull it out."

"Insurance?" asked the dealer.

"To be honest, I don't understand exactly what insurance is. The woman before you kept offering me that, and I never took her up on it."

"That means you can stake, on top of what you already plunked down, up to half your bet on the probability that I got a face card under here, which'd give me blackjack. We pay three to two odds on insurance. So, let's see, you got yourself about eight hundred bucks in there. That means you could stake another four hundred, and if I do have blackjack, you'd get six hundred back."

"So I'd be betting in the hopes that you've got me beat, in other words?"

"If you care to put it that way, sir."

"The logic of it all strikes me as pretty odd."

"The game does indeed have its oddities, sir."

The dealer had ditched his crusty Western twang and started sliding into the affected speech of an English butler. He was acting so polite and being so patient about explaining it all, Vic felt sure that he must have blackjack, and that the conversation therefore was entirely academic, since Vic didn't have any more money. Had the dealer looked at his down card yet? Vic couldn't recall. He eyed his neighbor's modest stack of chips.

"I'm down myself," said the cowpoke. "Otherwise I'd spot you a loan. As soon as you lose, I'm going to cash the rest of this in."

"I thought you said I might still pull it out on this hand."

"You might. Probably not, but who knows? I was just trying to offer some moral support there."

Vic turned to the dealer. "What if I don't have any more money?"

The dealer shrugged. "One must have money to purchase insurance, I'm afraid."

He sighed. "I suppose you all don't take credit cards."

"In Las Vegas they accept credit," said the dealer. "Here we adhere to a cash-only basis. Oasis is a cattle-ranching town, a cow town as the vernacular and the vox populi would have it, and we prefer to cleave to the old values that made the West what it is today. Rugged individualism and all that rot. That appears to be your own credo as well, sir, from what I've gleaned by eavesdropping on your conversation with the gentleman, so I'm sure you'll not take offence at my invoking it."

"In that case, I have seventeen."

"Blackjack," said the dealer.

Vic cracked his knuckles, a habit that had driven Andrea, his ex-wife-to-be, up a wall. She claimed that it would make fluid build up around his knuckles. He had only been able to refute her credibly when he happened across a Dear Abby column devoted to a similar dispute between two other star-crossed lovers. Abby cited a long-term study done between a control group and a group of knuckle poppers which proved that the knuckle poppers were generally less anxious and less likely to develop arthritis in their hands. Vic wondered whether they were also less likely to ram their own heads through a plate glass window, which is what he felt like doing.

Where had the hitchhiker gotten to? His fingers still felt tender from all the driving. He hadn't even gotten the chance to play that last hand. It really had been played by the cards themselves. That wasn't the way it had happened in *The Cincinnati Kid*. Steve McQueen at least got to suffer exquisitely from his tragic flaw, hubris or naivete or whatever it was. He, on the other hand, only felt bored, annoyed, vexed, empty, depressed, filled with rage and self-loathing at his own stupid-assed stupid stupidity.

"Let me buy you a drink," he heard himself saying. "Or actually, could you buy me one? All I have left is my five-dollar chip, and I'd like to hang onto that. Am I crying? My eyes are so red from all this driving and grit, it's hard to tell."

"Just a little," said the cowpoke. "A few manly, strangled tears, that's all, friend. I wouldn't even have noticed unless you'd asked me. Let's go to the bar. I think both of our friends have deserted us." The cowpoke strode along beside him, bearing down hard on his brass-headed cane and swinging his left hip with determination. "This cortisone has fucked me up royal. Dissolving my bones, is what it's doing. Back in Kentucky, where I used to live, the ground water has limestone deposits in it. That's what makes the thorough-breds' bones so strong. But if I went back to living there, the goldenrod pollen and the mold would kill me. I just can't win, friend. I can't buy an ace and I can't buy a life."

The voice of the dealer trailed them to the beaded curtain. "Jolly good show, old sport. Come again. Stiff upper lip. *Novus ordo seclorum.*"

The cowpoke in photosensitive glasses, whose name turned out to be Keith, ordered a light beer, and Vic had the same. "It's the only thing I drink," said Keith. "Medicinal. Thins out the mucous from my asthma attacks better than anything else. You know, you should have quit while you were up. They always pull the dealer switcheroo when a gambler's getting too far ahead. Kind of breaks your stride. Course my stride's already been broke, as you can see. Just a little joke there. By the way, how come your friend tried to kill me?"

"You must be mistaking me for somebody else."

"No, I'm not. I couldn't quite see your passenger, with that gun in his face, but I got a good look at you, since you were driving. I crushed my cellular telephone underfoot, and damn near ran off the road."

"I'm really sorry about that. My passenger has a radar gun that he likes to point at things. It's his toy, I guess. He's into relativity. But I don't think he meant to fire a shot at you."

"Well, it wouldn't be the first time somebody did. Besides, I know a thing or two about illegal weapons. I used to fence them a little bit, back in my salad days. That looked to me for all the world like a homemade shotgun. I guess I was feeling a mite nervous since I was just coming from the penitentiary. I buy tooled leather belts the prisoners make in shop there, as part of their rehabilitation, then I put Harley Davidson buckles on them, or death skulls, and sell them to bikers at flea markets in Arizona and Nevada. Those bikers can be some of the nicest fellows you'd ever want to meet if you catch them in the right mood. They don't haggle about the price. But boy, were the guards antsy around there today. Usually I come and go without too much fuss, it's a minimum security place, laid back, and they all know my face around there, but a prisoner escaped this morning.

They even strip-searched me and lifted out the spare tire in the back of my van before they let me leave. They always make me check my rifle before I go in, but this time I didn't think they were going to give it back to me."

"This morning, you say?"

"Yeah, some dude who's been in and out of there several times. He used to work out at Los Alamos on nuclear fusion or fission or whatever they call it, but then they caught him being a peeping tom, so that was a misdemeanor. Then it seems he scaled the fence at one of the nuclear test sites, a federal offense, so since he already had a record the district attorney pushed for a jail term and got it. But he's as harmless as you could want. Makes good belts, too. Burns some beautiful designs into them. Good with his hands."

"Shit." Vic lunged off his stool and raced to the door. The sudden glare of the afternoon light suffusing the inverted air made the objects in the parking lot hang back behind a scrim, but even before his vision made the adjustment, he knew the station wagon was gone. Negative space coalesced in a thick layer around the spot carved out where the car had sat, as if it had just that moment pulled away in the gravel, raising dust. The hitchhiker might have hot-wired it, if he was so good with his hands. Vic searched his pants pockets for the loose key and didn't find it. He could have sworn he'd taken it out of the ignition. "What's all the commotion?" Keith had followed him out, holding the cane aloft like a divining rod. The heat beat down with solid, elemental force. The cane was drawing the water out of Vic's body, drawing off the seventy percent of liquid that made up the human organism, leaving only a mummy, hollow, brittle and skeletal. "Losing all that money starting to get to you?"

"No, it's nothing. I haven't been taking in enough fluids on the road, and I feel a little weak. I shouldn't have drunk that booze. The guy you were just talking about is the same one I picked up as a hitchhiker, I'm pretty sure. He gave me the deed to a piece of land down in Baja. And now he's ripped off my car."

"The escapee? The fugitive? He must have recognized me when he came in the place, and cut out."

"I'm going to call the state police."

"Now wait a minute. No need to call the police, and get everybody stirred up."

"Everything I own was in that car. I can't just let him get away."

"I'll tell you what, I'll drive you back over to the penitentiary myself. I know exactly the person you'll need to talk to. I forgot to give them my order for next time, anyway. I was only running over here into Nevada to gamble a little, like I always do."

"I don't have any money left to pay for the lapsed registration anyway, even if they do recover it." Vic let himself crumple in a heap on the bed of gravel. "Besides, it'll probably fall apart by the time he gets to the under-ground chamber where his spaceship is hidden."

"How you doing, friend? I think you got yourself a touch of heat stroke. Let's hustle you inside. Course you already been hustled once today. Just a little joke there. We've got to move you into the shade."

"I don't know why Gamma Ray would go to the trouble of escaping. He was coming up for parole next month and was definitely going to get it. They'd already assigned him to my caseload." Her office was an aluminum-sided trailer with a foundation built under it, set a hundred yards or so away from the main buildings. It had orange shag carpet, a metal desk with a piece of cardboard stuck under one leg, and folding chairs that didn't match. A poster of the Eagles, off one of their old album covers, was taped completely over one window, so that the filtered daylight shone like numina around the assembled rock desperados. "You see that hole over there? They'd rather pump five thousand dollars worth of Freon and cold air through that hole than dispatch a carpenter over here with some lumber. It's no wonder they can't keep anybody in this job. The guy in it before me is working as a bouncer at a biker bar. He says he makes better money, the help is nicer, and the people he kicks out don't come back as often. Most of us are night-school MSW's, do-gooders with bad attitudes. I've stayed here longer than any of the men they hired, and that's because I pretty much tolerate their bullshit and their Level Two salary, as long as they let me do things the way I like."

Her name was Beth Wellington, but she said her parolees had nicknamed her Beef Wellington. She seemed expansive, not in a hurry, more eager to talk about herself than to ask him questions. She used to work on the Santa Fe railroad, first as a roustabout, then as a flagman and finally a switchman, until one night she was riding a caboose with the radio up full blast, hanging off the back so the engineer could watch her lantern signals, when the caboose switched onto the wrong track and plowed into a train oncoming at high speed. Beef was thrown seventy feet into a gully, not found for four hours, and had broken her bones and skull in more than thirty places. She'd lain in a ditch feeling the life seep out of her body, silently singing countless verses of John Henry to herself. Due to her altered state, she hadn't been able for the life of her to think of John Henry's name, so she'd substituted the name of the lead singer for the Eagles, Don Henley.

Nobody figured she would pull through, but when she was at the point of death, Mother Jones had come to her in a vision, had swooped up out of a coal shaft wearing clodhoppers, one of Beef's old flowered hippie dresses that she'd bought at the Salvation Army for a dollar, and a miner's hat with a carbon lamp on it. In the vision, Mother Jones said that a girl who'd gotten as far as she had in this line of work, in the face of all the ass-pinching and crude remarks of her co-workers, couldn't just give up the ghost, she had a lifetime of disability coming to her, and not to be a damn fool and squander what all those boys lying at the bottom of the collapsed seams of coal had worked so hard for. These were union-busting times, and every little bit of defiance counted for something.

So she recovered, as a gesture of worker solidarity, even though it meant sweating it out for several months in traction. After a couple of years of letting her bones knit and living solely off disability, Beef had gotten restless, drifted to Utah, and took up a less accident-prone line of work. She'd travelled here and somehow or other, though she kept saying she was going to quit, she stayed on. But she was starting to feel burned out on being a parole officer too. As hard as she worked to place her ex-cons in jobs, half of them ended up right back at the pen making five dollars a day turning out leather belts for Keith.

She needed to take a leave of absence now anyway, because the disability people in New Mexico had recently turned her up on a federal payroll sheet during an audit. Government bureaucracy moved slow but it moved all the same, now they were hassling her about working, and she wasn't about to sacrifice her compensation money for more of this paper-pushing grief. Around here, they didn't care if she truly rehabilitated anybody, as long as the numbers came out right and the Board of Prison Trustees didn't come breathing down their necks.

Prisons were built in out-of-the-way places for a reason, to mete out discipline where it wouldn't inconvenience the rest of the citizens, and this prison had a spotty reputation already. They were always threatening to close it down, so the warden didn't want any publicity, especially since the fugitive in question had escaped in broad daylight and hitched a ride practically right in front of the grounds. That was embarrassing, they would really look like goats if that came out, all thanks to Vic, so they were going to solve the matter as discreetly as possible with nobody the wiser who wasn't wise already. Not that she cared whether this jerkwater warden kept his job or not, he deserved to be turned out if the truth be told, but when crackdowns came, prisoner rights were the first thing to go.

And as worn down by the whole human recycling business as she was starting to feel, that was the last thing she needed right now. She'd tried to be an enlightened parole officer, but the years of service in a joint like this were starting to harden her in a way she didn't exactly like. If Vic really needed that car back right away, she could sympathize, but her advice, after reading his deposition, was that knowing the local redneck mentality around here the way she did, he shouldn't push his luck too hard. He hadn't committed a crime, exactly, by picking up Ray, or Gamma Ray, as the inmates all called him, though it could certainly be construed that way depending on who was doing the construing. And Vic wasn't going to earn the Governor's Commendation, however it fell out. Sometimes a misdemeanor could complicate your life a lot more than a felony. His best bet was to go on his way and wait for a form postcard telling him he could reclaim his stolen vehicle in such and such a place at his inconvenience.

"How do they plan to search for this Ray?" Vic wanted to know.

"I'm thinking I myself might just go look for him, off the record. I need a little paid vacation, to get those disability people in New Mexico off my tail. They owe me a lot of favors around this place, and opportunity has just knocked, for the first time since I came here. I threatened to resign a couple of months ago, so I think the warden will let me have my way, considering how hard up they are for decent replacements in this god-forsaken place."

"I think I may know where he is."

"Where?"

"Baja California. He gave me the deed to a lot he sort of owns, just before he ripped off my car. It's down past Ensenada, I don't know exactly where, but I have the latitude and longitude of it."

Beef took the deed from Vic's hand and studied it. "He'd be a fool to leave such an obvious clue, but then again, he's pretty much out of his mind to begin with. We've just recently strengthened our extradition treaty with Mexico. I do feel obliged to follow this lead, seeing as how it's the clearest one we've got." She sighed and gave Vic a long look. "You want to know something? I halfway hope for Gamma Ray's sake that he hits the border, abandons your car where we can find it easily, and keeps going."

"There are plenty of places beyond down there to hide out for life, if you're inclined that way. I'd like to find one myself."

"So would I."

"Belize, for instance."

"Great snorkeling there, I hear, with the coral reefs and all."

"Not to mention the seafood."

She had been pacing the length of the trailer. Her six-foot-plus frame had nowhere to go but five strides up and five strides back. When Vic got to his feet, they stood face to face, give or take a few inches. His mouth was close enough to her lips that he could have sneaked in one quick kiss before she decked him. It would be worth it for one taste of that hot, sweet mouth, with its faint aroma of dark-leaf tobacco.

"Ms. Wellington—"

"Call me Beef."

"Okay, uh, Beef. Keith has offered to give me a lift as far as Prescott, Arizona, where he lives. I'm going to work a couple of flea markets for him this weekend and pick up some pocket money, since I'm broke. We could all ride at least that far together, unless you were planning to drive down by yourself."

"No, I was going to take a bus. I'm a terrible driver." Beef turned away from him, and toward the window made translucent by the Eagles poster. She closed her eyes, seeming to commune with Don Henley again. The leader of the Eagles must have given her a satisfactory answer, for at last she opened her eyes and looked directly into his. "Since you're a party to the case, Vic, why don't you come down to Mexico with me?"

That evening she attended to the details of her departure on the bedroom telephone with the door shut. Vic spent the night on an army cot in a shared guest room of her house with Keith, listening to him snore. Vic hoped she didn't think that the noise was coming from him. When there was a lull, he could hear her sheets rustling in the room beside theirs.

The next morning she awakened, while Keith still whistled through his nose in the adjacent room, to find Vic already up, in the kitchen reading a newspaper several months out of date and drinking coffee out of a mustache cup at the formica table in one corner. "I hope you don't mind that I made a pot. I found an open can in the refrigerator, and this funky old cup was the only clean one. I didn't take yours, did I?"

"No, that's okay," she said, looking in a distracted way at the package of sausage in her hand, as if the two things were too much to think about at once so early in the day. "I meant to wash some last night. I guess I forgot." He decided to keep quiet and read the outdated news, in case she was a slow riser and needed time to fully wake up, but he found himself watching her movements.

She banged around the kitchen in panties and an oversized T-shirt, her legs so long they came to the top of the stove. She was frying up enough sausage in the iron skillet to make her place smell like a farmhouse. A window fan set next to the back door screen brought the cooler air in and blew around the sausage smoke. The heat of the day hadn't yet made itself felt, but a hint of the impending scorcher already hung in the air. "This time of year, I try to do all the day's cooking I'm going to before nine in the morning." Coming to her senses, and finding herself alone in her underwear with Vic, she seemed determined to keep up a stream of talk. He wondered why she didn't simply go get dressed first, and whether she did her housework in the nude when no one else was around.

"You never wash an iron skillet," she said, shaking flour straight from the bag into the bubbling grease. "Just wipe it with a dry cloth. That way it stays seasoned. Keith would make a fortune off me. I buy everything at the swap meets. This skillet cost me a dollar fifty. I got that mustache cup for a quarter."

"Did somebody with a mustache drink from it?"

"Who knows where it came from."

"I mean since you've owned it."

She tossed her uncombed hair back over her left shoulder—it seemed to be always her left—and gave the gravy a thoughtful stir. "Mhm. He used to wax the ends of his mustache. Twirl them up so he looked like a circus acrobat. At first I thought it was the most ridiculous thing I'd ever seen. I kept calling him Lars, but after a while I grew pretty fond of it. I never knew I'd feel so sad when he shaved it off."

"So, he doesn't live here now?"

Beef shrugged and took a puff off the cigarette she'd set down on the edge of the chipped enamel sink. It had a long ash on it, where she kept forgetting to smoke it. "I need to finish this before Keith gets up. The smoke bothers him. But I've got to have a cigarette in the morning before I eat, otherwise my food doesn't taste right." She turned off the gas and set the gravy on one of the back burners. The heat of the cast iron skillet kept it bubbling. "No, I guess he doesn't live here. It was one of those things where you keep trying to be friends, and keep making the mistake of sleeping with each other."

"It's an easy mistake to make. I've made it myself, once or twice."

"I hope you guys like canned refrigerator biscuits. That's the only kind I fix."

Vic took another sip from Lars's cup. "Those gummy ones? I love them. Whenever it was my turn to cook, my one specialty was tuna casserole with canned biscuits as the main ingredient. My turn kept getting less and less frequent, now that I think about it."

"Who took the other turn?"

"A gourmet."

"Female?"

"Yes."

"Did she have a mustache?"

"I didn't notice one. Well, maybe a cookie duster."

"Ah. I was hoping she had a Fu Manchu."

After the three of them finished breakfast, Beef drove back over to the penitentiary to speak with the warden and see to the details of her departure, making sure her caseload would be covered. Then she packed a single piece of soft luggage in half an hour, made a few final phone calls, closed up her little frame house with the torn screens and left the key with her elderly neighbor, who was outdoors wearing a bowtie with his short-

sleeved shirt and khaki shorts. Veins shone through his translucent legs in
the morning sun. The neighbor earnestly scattered crushed eggshells in his
railroad-tie flower bed with stiff arthritic jerks, as if he were in a piazza
tossing seed to birds at his feet. He didn't seem to understand exactly what
she was telling him about her possibly prolonged absence, but he took the
key in his palm and patted her arm all the same. "Ninety-seven years old,"
said Beef, "bones as brittle as balsa wood, and he still climbs up on his roof
to replace shingles every spring. I keep waiting for a big gust of wind to
carry him off. Bye Francisco," she shouted out the window at him, waving
as they pulled away. "I'll bring you back some seashells for your rock
garden if I get a chance."

Now they were humming along toward Prescott in Keith's van. "We'll
turn him up in our own sweet time," said Beef. "Sweet, sweet," she
repeated, lingering on the soft consonants. "Hey, do you remember the
Allman Brothers had a song called Sweet Melissa? It always made me wish
my name was Melissa." Vic rode in the passenger seat, and Beef reclined in
the van's back seat, her legs hanging over the end, her feet bare, her second
toe longer than the others. One of the van walls sported a gun rack, and in
it a Winchester rifle with a cherry-colored stock, one that Keith said he
used to use for squirrel hunting. The rifle was an issue from the sixties that
had been kept in beautiful shape, not a nick on it, and he'd bought it at an
auction in Bakersfield. Though he still had it licensed, he never took it
down much anymore, but he had a case of cartridges in the glovebox, and
kept the rifle oiled and took it apart to clean it every few months, just so it
wouldn't depreciate in value.

On the engine cover between the two front seats, Keith had placed a
plastic cooler filled with ice and light beer, so he could pop one open
whenever he suffered one of his frequent coughing fits. An alarming array
of inhalers was laid out in various compartments of the plastic tray on the
dash, along with piles of change sorted by denomination, time capsules,
miniature worry dolls, thimbles, wheat pennies, a Susan B. Anthony dollar,
butterscotch candy wrapped in gold cellophane. A stack of lottery tickets
protruded from the sun visor. The random yet meticulous arrangement of
the objects gave the dash area the aspect of a Buddhist shrine. Fishing idly
in the plastic tray, Vic picked up a carefully smashed, oval-shaped penny on
a trinket chain. Lincoln's burnished copper head had been elongated in the

extreme. It looked like the ritual deformations of skulls that Vic had seen on the mummified figures, swathed in crumbling woven funeral robes, in anthropological museums. "What exactly is this?" Vic asked, holding the deformed head aloft.

"Oh, you can get those pennies at flea markets and coin shows. I used to sell a lot of them. It's a novelty item."

"How do they get distorted this way?"

"I always heard they did it by setting them on a rail of the train tracks and letting the train cars run over them. At least that's what we told customers. Is that true, Beef? You ever run across any pennies on the tracks when you worked for the railroad?"

"That's probably what caused the caboose I was riding to derail and throw me down that gully. Some budding amateur scientist no doubt threw a penny across the rail just as we were backing up, to see what would happen." The landscape had given way to mesas, petrified pilings doing a slow geologic burn, massive outcroppings of rock that stood in stark isolation from their surroundings, exposing their naked layers of strata and the violent shifting of the earth's crust. The subtle continuum of color—desert rose, pink, and shale—marked eons, proterozoic, paleozoic, spores and gymnosperms, cycads and conifers, ginkgoes, ash, amphibians pressed into carbon. Late afternoon had flung its film of powdery light over the terrain, bringing out the igneous undertones of earth and rock, the ruddy gold sparkle of rubble, ore, and geodes.

In the oncoming lane, motorcycles two abreast, or in convoys, had been passing all day long, headed north. Most of them looked to be Harleys, choppers low to the ground, fitted for touring with extension forks, fairings, saddlebags, tapered gas tanks airbrushed with purple Vulcans and Thors whose chests and helmets glittered in gold-flake flames. As cycles ripped by, the butterfly baffles in their chrome mufflers pelted granite embank-ments with solid noise that came back in a cacophony of reverberations. The motorcycles kept passing, running into the hundreds, ridden by grim reapers in cracked leather jackets, lean and nasty, or graying longhairs of massive girth and Elvis sideburns whose perpetually pissed-off expressions could be detected even underneath their aviator shades. Many of them had women in tow, cushioned on the hard seats by rumps squeezed without mercy into tight black jeans, their thick midriffs and sagging bosoms barely contained by string tops. The women's hair whipped in a tangle about taut faces as their lashes batted back tears. They stared down passing cars with defiant, red-rimmed expressions.

"Where in God's name are all those bikers headed? Are they Hell's Angels? I don't remember seeing so many motorcycles when I first started East a week or so ago."

"They're not attending the harmonic convergence, that's for sure," Beef offered from her languorous repose in the back seat, lifting the curtain from the van's side window with her second toe.

"They're on their way to a chopper pow-wow in Dakota, up around the Badlands," said Keith. "It starts in a week or so. They make gypsy encampments along the way, at rest stops or state parks, or just find a big empty patch of land off the road and pitch tents. Thousands of bikers from all over the country go. I keep promising myself I'm going to take a mess of leather belts up there. I'd make a killing. I always pick up some side business this time of year from some of the ones who come through Phoenix on their way to the Grand Canyon. But there sure are a lot more on the road this year than I've ever seen before."

When they took a break for dinner, their roadside choices were a restaurant advertising *Food—Stop Now*, and a Basque-American cafe that served authentic cuisine family style. They chose the Basque-American cafe, cram-packed with people at trestle tables. They were shown to three empty seats amongst a multitude consisting of a middle-aged man at the head, with burst blood vessels in his cheeks, who sported a beret and a squarish beard; four adult women in kerchiefs and dresses that buttoned down the front; and children who squirmed, poked each other, grabbed unleavened bread out of the baskets in the center of the table, and whispered to one another in phrases that sounded vaguely biblical. "I didn't know there were Basques around here," Vic said to the waitress as she set down a glass of water in front of him.

"Yep. This corner of the world is overrun with them," she answered, making rapid calculations on her pad as if she planned to give him an exact count. "They've got quite a little enclave here, that goes back all the way to last century. One begets two, two beget four." Vic wondered what the relationship among the inhabitants of his table could be. Were these members of a polygamous Basque clan? He didn't know anything about

Basque-Americans. Did they live in communes? Maybe everybody was a survivalist in this latitude.

The waitress returned and set down a large ceramic bowl of alphabet soup, obviously out of a can, and three smaller empty bowls. As she ladled the soup, taking care not to spill any drops, Vic could see Keith and Beef trying to suppress laughter by coughing into their hands. Their punchiness was starting to affect him too, and his chest heaved, but he managed to contain himself as the waitress explained that they didn't have to order, it was all family style, and she would return in a few moments with the second course.

"Authentic cuisine," said Beef, her eyes wide in mock appreciation and wonderment as she held aloft the smoking spoon she'd removed from her mouth.

"This must be the American part of the eating experience," said Vic. "The sign did say Basque-American." The three of them shook and hiccuped with laughter, trying to choke it back when they drew looks of consternation from the tribe occupying most of the table. Vic couldn't swallow the salty soup. His stomach had shrunk over the past week, and was now in spasms from giggling, so he stared hard into the vegetables and noodles in his bowl, trying to look as if he was saying grace. The Basque patriarch had made a sizeable dent in his main course already, slicing repeatedly into a hunk of rare roast lamb, seared on the outside, and chewing the pieces with gusto. He probably had to consume a lot of protein so that he could keep up his stamina, service his various wives, propagate the species and spread his seed over the earth. Leaning back into his chair betweeen bites to contemplate his flock, the man, with his burst blood vessels, had the rosy, placid, self-satisfied posture of a husband and father finishing off another productive day, at peace with himself and right before God and man.

The ball of sun on the horizon sent its blinding orange last beam of radiation shooting straight through the plate glass into Vic's peripheral vision, then slipped behind a bluing jagged peak as photons scattered along his retina. The corona of light the sun left behind simmered. Letters floating in the bowl of alphabet soup reclaimed his attention, their outlines sharp and glossy. He could make out words being formed, *cur* and *sod* and *fib*. Was he having a mystical experience? Or was he just spazzing out again? He stole a glance at Beef's bowl of soup. She didn't seem to have any discernible words floating in hers. On the contrary, she licked her spoon, letting it slide from her mouth, giving him irrefutably scorching looks, with meanings not the least bit difficult to decipher. His soup might turn cold before he ate it, but she, in full possession of her appetites, wasn't about to let him get cold feet on the pretext of ambiguous body language.

Or was he misreading her too? Maybe she simply felt playful at the outset of her journey. Every toss of her head, every flash of the one dimple on the right side of her face, every crinkle of her crow's feet, every open and close of those chapped but voluptuous lips put him in mind of Andrea, even though the two women had absolutely nothing in common. He found himself aching for Andrea now, in a complicated way, one that had something to do with a recurring dream he used to have for a while after things started to go badly between them, a dream about stopping off at the store on his way back from the university to pick up a quart of buttermilk for a bread recipe she was making and getting stuck in traffic on El Camino, at that left turn signal that always took an eternity to change, then nuclear bombs started to fall on the campus, and he knew as the outline of the mushroom cloud started to take shape over the eucalyptus grove behind the cinder track that he wouldn't be able to get back to Andrea at the cottage.

He'd wanted to see her once more, to say their final goodbyes and to show her that he really hadn't forgotten this time, that was his favorite bread and he'd made a point of writing himself a note about the buttermilk, wrapping it around the keyring in his pocket so he wouldn't forget, and he even would have gotten home at the hour agreed upon except for that wretched turn signal, and now that they were both about to be obliterated forever, she would carry her skepticism and anger to the grave. He would never be able to prove to her that the buttermilk had indeed been in the back seat at the final moment, lying on its side, still chilled inside the paper sack, beaded with sweat. A hand touched his hand and he awoke, shaking with cold. "I need to make a phone call," he blurted out, pushing back his chair.

"Don't let me stop you," Beef answered softly, her voice patient, uncurious, sure of itself.

It would have put him in the best light at this juncture, he figured, to simply turn and stride away from the table, cocksure and inscrutable, but it occurred to him that he didn't have any pocket money whatsoever, that he was running a tab for his living expenses until Keith could get some work out of him. He could try using his calling card access number, but he had his doubts whether the long-distance computer would accept it. "I don't suppose one of you could forward me a little cash, could you?"

"I don't know how much you need for a phone call, but take some change out of the dashboard tray in the van," said Keith, throwing him a keyring. "You can pay me back later."

"Thanks. I'm in your debt. I mean, I was already in your debt, and now I'm even deeper in your debt." He baubled the keyring as if it had been a hot baked potato, and deposited it in his pocket. The man at the cash register, probably the owner, on his feet keeping watch over the clientele with folded arms and the alert, no-nonsense eyes of a pit boss, informed him that the restaurant didn't have a pay phone, but the new motel under construction next door probably did, if it was open. Vic stumbled across the lamplit asphalt to the van, scooped a handful of change into his pocket, and stepped over the curb separating the two places of business.

The spanking poured concrete of the motel parking lot shone white as a bleached skull under the halogen lights. Even the fresh clumps of dirt lying scattered at the edges seemed repelled by the limpid surface. Strings of plastic pennants, red, blue, and yellow, stretched across the building's facade, hanging still in the windless night, awaiting the grand opening. The wooden skeleton of only one wing remained to be covered, but the rest had been stuccoed in Spanish style, with Moorish arches. No one was in the lobby, but passing through it, he came into an open courtyard, paved with flagstones. At the far end of it stood a glassed-in solarium, housing a swimming pool illuminated by underwater lights. An old man with stooped shoulders stood at the shallow end, fishing in the water, using a long aluminum pole with a mesh net attached to one end.

It took several phone calls and about half his change, first to information, then to the Horace Academy, where he talked someone fortunately working after hours into releasing the phone number and address of an employee by telling her he was Andrea's half-brother. Then he dialed a friend of hers where she was supposed to be staying, then the place where she'd actually relocated, before he at last connected with Andrea's voice. "Vic?" He heard the suppressed emotion in her tone, and realized that for her, as for most people, getting a call from him at any time was like getting a call from a normal person at four in the morning. No matter how under control the caller attempted to sound, no matter how light and bantering to set you at your ease, the mere fact of the call put you on edge, and you couldn't let your breath escape until you knew the full extent of the disaster so you could at least begin the process of grieving.

"Yes, it's me. Don't worry, nothing's wrong. I just got to thinking about you, for no reason in particular, and I wanted to see how you were settling into your new job."

"Oh. Hm, well, it's okay. It's had its ups and downs. But the teaching is going better than I figured it would. The students were eager to please, anyway. Once I got over the initial stage fright." He could hear a voice in the background, talking rapid-fire with giddy emphasis. The television, with any luck.

"Am I interrupting anything?"

"No. I mean, not anything that I can't get back to later. And what about your new job?"

"Well, my week's had its ups and downs, too," he said. "It's turned out a little different than I expected."

"Are they all nouvelle professionals who talk about rent control and Montessori? I can imagine you'd have a hard time fitting into that crowd. I know how that kind of stuff gets to you. But you might have kids yourself some day. Montessori does have its good points, just remember that. Regimented iconoclasm." She laughed spontaneously, a pure oxygen flash of the old Andrea.

"I've really been missing you, Andrea. I think I may have made a big mistake."

He listened to her indrawn breath; shallow and fast, she was almost panting. Against all probability, he had caught her in a vulnerable mood, melancholy and nostalgic like him, yearning to be touched. He had expected to find her hard, not by her nature but out of necessity, a healthy survival instinct. "Be careful, Vic," she said. "Talk isn't cheap anymore. A month ago you could say whatever you wanted, risk any sweet nothing that entered your head, and I was all ears."

"I'm not just talking. I mean what I'm telling you. I want us to be together. The last couple of days, I keep reliving little bits of our shared life. It dawned on me how all along I took the intensity of your love for granted, and squandered something precious. I know these are all cliches, and that Pushkin would say it a lot better, throw in lots of irony and daredevil witticisms in perfect hexameter, with feminine rhymes and all. But I'm in a funk. I'm dead tired, and I want to say it all plain, unvarnished, so you'll know I'm not playing with you. I love you."

"I don't know." Her voice brimmed, almost tearful. "You've got me pretty confused, I have to tell you. This is exactly the way I've wanted you to say those things all along, like a total sap, without any brilliant tropes. I told them at the school not to give my number out in case you called. So I wasn't expecting to pick up the phone here in San Diego and find you at the other end."

"Are you saying yes, then?"

"You want me to move to New York with you? It's hard to think about that prospect, after I've barely started this new job. Last week I signed a lease on a cottage down here in San Diego. They've overbuilt like crazy, and the rental rates are really good, but once they get your signature on the contract they're desperate for you to stay."

"Andrea, does it seem to you like there are more unoccupied dwellings than ever before? In history, I mean."

"I'm not sure I understand what you mean. This isn't one of those questions of yours, is it?"

"No. Forget I said it."

"Anyway, I'd at least have to finish out the semester."

"Maybe you wouldn't have to relocate right away. I could join you out there until you can get things squared away. I feel like time is running out. I have to come right now, tonight. I'll make a living in the meantime, I promise you. I can sell cans of cold beer to the boogie boarders on the beach, if it comes to that."

"But what about your job? I'm sure they won't be exactly thrilled if you up and quit so soon. Even if you switch to another firm, you want to be able to count on a good letter of reference. Don't do anything rash, Vic. I know how you get. Don't burn your bridges, okay? Let's take a few days to think over the specifics calmly, without haste. But I want you to know that it means a lot to me, for you to open yourself up this way. I'm really touched by it. I'm going to go take a long walk on the beach tonight, and have a

good cry about it, and I want you to go to that little place down in the
Village with the stupid opera music on the jukebox that serves black walnut
cheesecake with glazed caramel topping, and have a double portion. One
for you, and one for me. Are you close to it? I imagined that you'd find a
studio somewhere around there, you always have great luck turning up the
very best places for bottom dollar, even if you can't manage to keep them.
It's so strange hearing your voice long distance. You know what I mean?
Romantic and sad. I kind of like it. I wish I could be in your arms right
now. Maybe we should each stay on our separate coasts, so you can call me
up and I can listen to you talk. Are you calling from a public phone? I
thought I heard you feeding coins into a slot. At first I wasn't sure, because
it's amazingly quiet on your end. I don't know of a single phone booth in
Manhattan where it ever gets that quiet. But the background static makes it
sound like you're surrounded by space, cavernous space. Are you standing
on a wharf by the Hudson River?"

"That's what I wanted to talk to you about. See, I'm not exactly in
Manhattan."

"Not in Manhattan? Where are you, then?"

"Arizona. At least I think it's Arizona. It could still be Nevada, or
Utah." Now the silence opened out on her end. Even the television, or
whoever it was, had fallen as mute as her. The next words out of her mouth
would probably be Let the grieving begin. "Don't be angry, Andrea. I still
mean everything I said. A few things happened to me en route to New
York. Nothing irreparable, and it doesn't have to affect our plans for a life
together."

"What things, Vic? Precisely what things?"

"I had an anxiety attack in New Jersey, so I decided to drive back to
California. Then I picked up a hitchhiker, sort of a—a fanatic, I guess you'd
call him. Although he did argue his point of view with a lot of per-
suasiveness, judging him strictly on a forensic basis. Anyway, he stole your
car while I was in a backwater casino trying to build us up a nest egg. Well,
backwater is just a figure of speech, because there was no water anywhere in
sight, and I suffered a mild heat stroke. I'd been forgetting to eat and drink,
otherwise I don't think the heat would have gotten to me. It turns out that
the hitchhiker had escaped from federal prison earlier in the day. I honestly
didn't know he was a fugitive, because even I wouldn't have been that

imprudent. I'm really sorry about the car, Andrea. If they don't recover it, I'll get you another one, a later model. It's too bad, because I'd just put a new radiator in it the day before."

"I don't want the car back, Vic. I gave it to you. Don't you remember? It's your legal responsibility now. And I also don't want to hear any more about your adventures."

He started to correct her, but was interrupted by an electronic voice instructing him to please deposit another eighty-five cents. The voice was a plausible simulacrum, even if the intonation was a little off, and he would have obeyed it, but he had come to the end of his change. He searched his pockets in vain. "Andrea, I don't have any more money. All I can find is a five-dollar poker chip. Could you call me back? Let's see, they must have the number written on here somewhere. Yeah, here it is. The area code is 602, and the number is eight seven five, one three one three. Did you catch that, honey?" The line had gone dead. The protracted twilight had dissolved, leaving the stars to shine. There was the Big Dipper, hanging aloft, one of the few constellations he could pick out. Andrea knew them all, Orion, the Pleiades. The old man in the illuminated solarium still fished in the turquoise pool, making broad but meticulous sweeps with his long aluminum pole, bringing out nothing, not even a pocket of silt. "Hey!" a voice called out from somewhere in the shadows. "Spear the tarpon! Knock off what you're doing already, and spear the tarpon!"

The old man lifted out his net, set it with slow care on the concrete, and turned his long, searching, disappointed stare on the depths of the pool. He didn't appear to see any tarpon. With his hunched shoulders and down-trodden air, he looked like a woodsman who'd just found out that in the deceptively clear waters of his favorite mountain lake all aquatic life, down to the last shred of algae, had been obliterated by acid rain. He picked the aluminum pole back up and resumed sweeping the pool.

Long minutes passed. Maybe she'd gone to take that walk on the beach and have a good cry. He couldn't say he blamed her. All the same, he loitered. The phone rang, and he let it ring three more times, just to hear the sound of it reverberate in the still desert night, with its luxuriant profusion of stars. He picked up the receiver. "Hello, Andrea."

"I want you to listen to me. You've got me so choking on my bile that I can barely talk. But I'm going to have my say. You fucked me over, Vic.

Just when I thought I was beyond your reach, and you couldn't hurt me anymore, you went and opened me wide up and fucked me over again."

"You think I called you up to hurt you?"

"No, I honestly think your intentions were quite the opposite. What I used to like about you is that you're not a smooth operator. Every guy I went out with before you was an operator. I really got sick of that. But now I find out that the net effect is the same. In your own charming, klutzy way, you've completely messed my mind as much as any other GQ with an IQ. I could imagine living with you under certain circumstances. You bring excitement into my world. I never know what's coming next. You don't have me on the phone two minutes, and I'm practically swooning. But I've had enough calamity for this decade. Until you get your head together, I don't want to receive any more phone calls from the lonesome prairie."

"But I will make good, that's what I'm telling you. As long as it's something else besides law. I was thinking that you and I could go live in Baja California together. I wanted it to be a surprise, kind of spruce it up first, but I might as well go ahead and tell you. Right before he stole my car, the inmate gave me a coupon that can be redeemed for the deed to a piece of land down there. We could fix it up, build a cottage. It's supposed to be some sort of planned retirement community, I think, but I have a feeling we'd be the only ones there, at least for a few years. It could turn out so beautiful, Andrea. You know how much we both love the beach."

"A coupon, Vic? A coupon from an escaped convict?"

"I know what you're thinking. But I do know how to read legal contract language, give me that much credit. Let's at least go take a look at it before we make up our minds. It can't be more than two days' drive, max, from where you're standing. Look, if it means that much to you for me to have a profession, I'll go back and finish an MD in sports medicine before we settle down there. It wouldn't take that long. I've accrued tons of college credits that I haven't done anything with. They're like a bank account just sitting there, waiting to be useful."

"I don't want to live in Baja. Why would I want to live in Baja California?"

"Okay then, I'm flexible. But let's do something extraordinary. The stars are out tonight, and the sky's the limit. We could set up a clinic right here in Arizona, or Nevada—wherever this is. Right here where I'm standing, you probably can't find a decent doctor within a hundred miles. Everybody I meet out here seems to have some kind of ailment or affliction. All different ones, too. I'll bet these Basques don't get proper medical care, and with the kind of high-cholesterol diet they eat, they're at definite risk for coronary artery disease. I'm not sure whether their religion allows them to receive medical treatment, but we could make inquiries."

"Which is it going to be, Vic? Arizona? Baja? Sports medicine? Law? Month before last you were going to throw it all over to become a foreign correspondent. You're an attorney. That's what you are. When people ask you at cocktail parties what you do, that's what you must tell them. You're not due for a mid-life crisis yet. And you're certainly not scheduled to go live in a retirement community the same week you're supposed to be starting your first real job. For once in your life you've actually finished something, except for the bar exam, and now you have to practice it, even if it kills you. Otherwise, I can't see any possibility of living with you. I want an airtight arrangement or nothing. Your deadline for options and second thoughts passed about six weeks ago. Maybe I'm strange this way, maybe it's fallen out of fashion, but I want a happy life, without any complications besides the normal ones. I don't want to be around you when you end up as a bartender in the Florida Keys with facial tics and an atrophied degree."

"I know you're right, in a way. And I really did try to go to New York. But I can't. I literally can't."

"Why not? What is it that's getting you down? These past few months, you've been acting peculiar and threatening to drop out. You've always been a little bit that way, at least since I've known you, but your eccentricities have gotten worse. And whenever I ask you about it, you say it's nothing."

"I can't explain it. But I can't go work for that firm, or any other one. Every time I even think about it, I get physically sick."

"Then we don't have anything else to talk about. Things are going well for me here, and I don't feel like working myself up into the state of nerves I was in before I came down here. Summer session's over, and I have a couple of weeks break before I have to start back in."

"That's good to hear, Andrea. I really mean that. You made the right choice when you left me. I shouldn't have called you. I lost my head. But if you do happen to change your mind in the next couple of days, I'll be in

Prescott, Arizona, working at a flea market. Should I give you the number? I can run next door and get it."

"No. And Vic, I assume that if you actually carry thorugh with this latest half-baked idea, you'll be passing through here on your way to Baja. Please don't show up on my doorstep. I know how you get carried away by your enthusiasms."

"All right. I promise I won't. Goodbye, then."

"Vic?"

"Yeah?"

"Do you need any money? Like bail, I mean. I didn't ask whether you were in jail on account of the escaped prisoner business. I don't know exactly how that sort of thing works, legally. I thought this might be your one phone call, and that in your delirium you forgot to mention it. That's why I called back. If you need somebody to post bail, I can come up with the cash."

"No, I'm all right. Thanks anyway. I was the victim, it appears."

"Okay. So long, Vic. Keep well. Or as well as you can."

"Bye, honey."

He hung up. Another employee had thrust his head into the doorway of the solarium and was talking to the pool sweeper. "I been yelling at you to spread the tarp on, you old coot. You hard of hearing or something? We need to get out of here. Do you want to eat at Food Stop Now, or the Basque place?"

As they plummeted and rose in darkness toward Keith's town, Vic lay in the back seat with his head on Beef's lap, feeling the road unfold in serpentine turns beneath him and looking up at the van's ceiling with his eyes open while she stroked his forehead and cheeks.

"I know these roads like the back of my hand," Keith kept saying between swigs of beer, as he took one hairpin curve after another at high speed. "You go off the side of one of these mothers, with no guard rail, and you've got a long way to fall." Keith gave a running monologue about the landscape they were passing, telling them what they would have been seeing if it had been daylight.

"Hardly anybody ever comes to these little side canyons, cause everybody's so cranked up about seeing the great big famous hole, but the smaller canyons are pretty impressive in their own right. Fellow around here who works for the college over at Flagstaff was telling me a big meteorite shower came a few hundred million years ago and dug a bunch of these canyons right out. How'd you like to been standing around barbecuing your mastodon when that happened, hey?" Once in a while he'd punctuate his observations by remembering horrible wrecks he'd witnessed at certain places along the highway. "Some of the Mexicans and Indians even put markers down, white crosses and piles of stones, when it's their relatives. You never actually see the bereaved, but somebody comes out here real early and puts bunches of fresh flowers by the markers every now and again." Keith's voice was pleasant, a local news station turned to at random late at night to keep from falling asleep, the sound kept down low as the litany of disasters is recited. Beef bent her neck and let the long black strands of her hair fall into Vic's face. He raised his head up, having to strain a little in his awkward position, and kissed her full on the mouth. She hadn't lit a cigarette since breakfast, perhaps in deference to Keith, but the sweet and smoky tang of dark cured tobacco still lingered in her saliva.

When the van at last slowed, then stopped, leaving a sudden quiet in its void, Vic raised up to see where they were. "Getting close to home now," said Keith. They were backed up in traffic, five or six vehicles ahead of them, on a stretch of desolate county road. After they'd sat for a few minutes, Vic opened the sliding door and hopped out to see what the holdup was. Keith kept fidgeting, looking into his sideview mirror, and into the one on the passenger side that said *Objects Closer Than They Appear*. The only objects in sight behind them were a slash of road, crimson in the reflected taillights, and twists of rabbit scrub and locoweed.

Keith switched off the ignition, and they got out. The three of them made their way up to the front of the line of traffic along the graded shoulder. Keith heaved along on his cane, muttering alliterative curses that had to do with shit and shinola, frigging and frog gigging, and Beef and Vic walked behind with their arms around each other so as not to trip. Two state police motorcycles had formed a roadblock, blue strobes flashing, and the policemen, on foot but still wearing helmets, had set out triangles and were holding up highway flares, the cores of orange light flaming up between the pulses of blue.

47

A cowboy appeared from behind the silvery glint of the roadside sagebrush, astride a horse that he checked in the middle of the highway, as it shied from the flares and strobes. There followed a trotting line of spotted cows that slowly began to cross the road, swinging their flanks, a caravan. In the artificial glare against the dark background of their hides, the broad, shifting, irregular patches of white looked like maps of land bridges and continental drift.

"Is this the real thing?" Vic asked. "Or are they shooting a movie?"

"Oh, that's a real cowhand all right. Most of them nowadays work giving canyon rim rides for the tourist trade. But we still got a few bona-fide ones out here. They must have fallen behind schedule herding them back from grazing." The haunches of the cows pitched upward as each one reached the other side of the highway and ran down the embankment into the surrounding darkness.

"Do you think there are more cows than ever before? On earth, I mean."

"I don't know much about the inner workings of the cattle trade. Me and a buddy did plow into a heifer once, in my old pickup truck, after we'd been up to Reatta Pass drinking. We were drunk as skunks, and putting the pedal to the metal. Came around a curve and there she was in the middle of the road, relaxed as you please, and she looked as big as Paul Bunyan's Babe to me as I tore into her. Banged my truck up royal. Crushed that front end like a beer can. We did get to keep the meat, at least. That's the law, you know. They got lots of peculiar laws on the books out here, some leftover from frontier times. Does seem like everybody and his cousin has got a little spread these days. Boutique ranches, we call them. I don't know why they're so popular, since the wholesale price of the meat keeps going down. Some kind of global glut, must be, like you say. The three of us may as well get back in the van to stay warm. We could be here all night, and desert nights at this altitude do get chilly."

When they finally pulled into the driveway of Keith's house, a little suburban ranch-style with aluminum siding, sitting among a cluster of similar houses that looked like they'd dropped out of the sky into a big field, it was late enough that a thin coat of dew had formed on the stubble of lawn. Dewdrops saturated Vic's canvas shoes as he helped carry wicker baskets to the front porch. Keith wanted to go in first, to open the windows for them and let the house air out, but Beef said she was about to bust. "Down and the first door to the right," said Keith. Finding himself alone at the sliding door of the van with Keith, Vic laid his arm on Keith's and whispered "Thanks for not saying anything about me and the girlfriend I mentioned maybe going down to Baja with. Things are sort of in flux."

"No problema. I got enough worries of my own without mixing in yours. Me and Beef go back a pretty good ways. She puts me up in that spare room of hers now and again. I'm glad to finally have a chance to reciprocate. She's about the only person I know who can stand to be within earshot of my disgusting barnyard noises when I sleep. My second ex-wife sure couldn't, after my condition started getting bad. It's improved a little bit here recently, believe it or not. Time was I got weak as a puppy, and could barely roll over in bed."

"She's very fond of you, it's obvious."

"Oh, I don't know. We're not what you'd call real close these days—I only see her when I go over to the prison to buy stuff—but we got what you might call an understanding. So you be nice to her. She's been needing somebody to treat her good for a long time."

When they were inside, Keith began to apologize for the looks of his house. "You all will have to excuse the mess. This is the way a bachelor lives. I work out of my home, and the second bedroom, along with the living room and kitchen, serves as my warehouse. We'll have to clear a space for the two of you to sleep on the twin bed in there." He said this offhand, without looking at either of them.

The pegboard walls of the bedroom were hung with antique razor strops or butchering instruments of some type, maybe ones used long ago in a barbershop or slaughterhouse, and corrugated metal washboards of all different sizes, stamped with advertisements. *Barclay's Pure Pear Elixir Refreshes and Invigorates. Its Medicinal and Purgative Powers Are Undisputed. Treats Scabies, Rabies, Unwanted Babies.* Trick iron coin banks stared out from various shelves about the room—clowns with features like the faces of gorgons, eyebrows unfurling, eyes popping, iron ringlets standing out from the skull in rigid, snaky coils, huge red lips, gapped mouths and protruding tongues at the ready to swallow any coin placed in the slotted hands. The four-poster bed, piled with boxes of carnival glass and rolls of tissue paper, had a bedspread patterned with some indeterminate animal.

"It's cozy," said Vic.

"Cozy as a torture chamber," said Beef. "You need an interior decorator worse than I do, Keith."

"I hear you, I hear you. If I'd known beforehand I was going to have visitors, I could have softened the decor a little bit. Made it into more of a B and B type place." Keith cradled one of the iron banks in the crook of his left arm. "Now you'll notice the good detail work on these. Some of the factories that specialize in reproductions use the same mold over and over thousands of times, until the features of the last ones to come off the gummed-up mold get completely worn down. I only deal in quality goods myself. That's an antique bed, New England maple, circa 1780. And this Barbie doll—" he held up a cardboard box for inspection, Barbie mounted upright in her oblong cellophane encasement, in cryonic splendor, sea-blue eyes open in wonderment and anticipation, the stiff ponytail and tapired legs untouched. "Ain't she beautiful? One of the original issues. You get one of these babies in mint condition, like this one here, it'll fetch over a thousand dollars. Well, I'll let you all get some shuteye. I need to lie down and give my poor alveoli a rest. Night."

"Night, Keith. Sleep tight. Don't let the scorpions bite."

They sat on the edge of the cleared bed, their hands crossed in their laps, and heard his door shut across the hall. "Alone at last," said Vic. After a moment of silence, Keith's room exploded in blaring, distorted dialogue. Some late-night TV show or other, it was impossible to tell with the volume up so high. "How's he going to sleep with that on? He really needs to get some rest."

Beef removed her hoop earrings with quick dipping motions of her head, as if she were shaking water from her ears. "These things are killing me. I don't wear them often, so the skin starts to grow back. I need to have my earlobes pierced again. The question is, how are we going to sleep with that on? He's used to it. When he stays in motels, which is most of the time, he probably blasts his neighbors out so they won't hear his snoring. He's kind of self-conscious about it, and assumes it gets on everybody's nerves. I'm sure he thinks we feel more private listening to an earsplitting rerun of *Creature From the Black Lagoon* instead of him. It's his funny way of being considerate."

The twin bed with its high maple bedposts was too narrow for them, so they had to lie on their sides. She found his mouth again, and they kissed. "Melissa," he said. "Sweet Melissa."

"It does sound nice, doesn't it."

Her kisses were hard and searching. Vic guessed that her body's movements would be slow and lazy, domestic, the way Andrea's always were when he'd managed to arouse her early in the morning. But Beef was unbuttoning his shirt, tugging at the buckle on his belt, running her hands over his chest. "Whoa there. If thou'rt going to be mine own wedded wife, thou must first apprise me of that which I most yearn to know."

"What's that? Whether I'm still a virgin?"

"I want to know if you do housework in the buff."

"That's a little personal, don't you think, considering how little I know about you?"

"Dear Abby says it's a socially acceptable activity. As long as the curtains are drawn, it's a matter of individual choice."

"You read Dear Abby?"

"That's what I was looking for in that old newspaper of yours this morning."

"You talk too much. Stop clowning around and fondle me."

He slipped his hands underneath her blouse and found her breasts. She must have removed her brassiere when she'd gone into the bathroom before. His caresses were tentative, tender, but Beef pressed her body forward, urging him to stroke her with a firmer touch. The taut flesh around her belly had what looked like faded stretch marks, or maybe faint scars from her accident long ago. He ran his fingers over the marks, touched his lips to them, and unzipped her jeans. She raised her bottom to make it easier for him to slide the jeans off. Using his tongue like a cat's, he tried to give her pleasure in slow laps, grazing the folds right at the top with his lower lip, the way Andrea had liked, and ran his fingertips up and down her sides. She squirmed in what he took for enjoyment, clutching the hair on the back of his head until the roots hurt, and after a while she began to pull him up toward her by his hair.

When he resisted, she sat up. "As you can probably tell, I'm horny as hell and about to go off my rocker, so I don't need elaborate stimulation. I appreciate the technique, sugar, but why don't you take your pants off and come right on in? The water's fine."

"Okay," he said, fumbling with his zipper. "I just thought you might want a little foreplay."

"As far as I'm concerned, the foreplay started about a hundred miles back, when you lay your head down in my lap. I was ready to sing the Star Spangled Banner right then. You may be accustomed to getting laid on a regular basis, but it's been a long dry stretch for me with nothing but my Eagles posters and a memory that gets a lot of exercise. I don't exactly meet the most eligible bachelors in my line of work. And you can imagine how cosmopolitan the social life is after hours at Utah's fabulous rural watering holes."

"I hadn't thought about that," he said, removing one sock and toying with it.

She embraced him from behind and pressed her nose against the nape of his neck. "What is it? Are the farm implements and the television getting to you? How about a massage?"

"It isn't that. I haven't been completely forthright. During dinner, when I went to make that phone call, it was long distance to the woman I used to live with. I haven't quite straightened out that part of my life yet."

"Is that all?" She laughed a belly laugh. "You really do have scruples. From the look on your face just now, I thought it might be something serious. Listen, Vic. I could care less about whatever ghosts you have lurking about. Don't you think it felt odd for me too, to have you sitting at my kitchen table this morning, drinking out of that mustache cup? You even slurp your coffee the way he used to."

"I slurp my coffee?"

"Yes, you do. But don't worry, because I can live with it. I did live with it. All I want right now, tonight, to put it bluntly, is to hump you and be humped by you. We'll take the rest as it comes. You've got a nice little bod on you, and I plan to enjoy it. I hope you're not going to disappoint me by telling me that you really and truly invited me along because you wanted to be a good citizen and help me look for Gamma Ray."

"No. I guess if I'm honest with myself, I was mostly hoping to get into your pants."

"Well, unfortunately I don't happen to have them on right now. But why don't you grope around and see what else you can find?"

He climbed up on the bed. When he slipped inside, she was so engorged it gave him a shiver. With one arm she pinned him fast to her breast, while the other hand roamed over his buttocks. As he struggled against her, twisting his head, she nipped the tender flesh along the front of his neck over and over.

Afterward, a breeze blew in from the open window drying the sweat on their soaked heads. He was going to sleep more peacefully than he had in a long time. He lay there in her arms, she in his, and feebly fought off the drowsy stupor stealing over him, so he could prolong the moment of bliss.

"That didn't hurt, did it?"

"No, it was good. Strange, but good." Her hand moved under the sheet, not deliberate, idly groping. "Give me a few minutes," he said. "You're insatiable."

"Not insatiable. Just not sated. When I am, you'll know. Then I start to act like a hibernating she-bear. I'm not to be messed with."

"Somehow, you don't strike me as having a mean streak in you."

"I'd reserve judgement on that until you know more about me."

"Okay, I will." He lazily stroked her backside with the arm that wasn't pinned under him. "Anyway, I do feel like I know you."

"How do you figure?"

"I know you have to smoke a cigarette in the morning, otherwise your food doesn't taste right. I know your second toe is longer than your big toe."

"Keep going."

"I know you do all your cooking before nine in the summers, you only make canned biscuits, you take a while to wake up, so I'd better tiptoe if I'm the first one awake tomorrow. You always toss your hair over your left shoulder. I've been acquainted with people for years, people I supposedly cared about heart and soul, without knowing that much about them. I feel so damn good right now. I don't give a shit about anything."

"Mm. Me neither." She snuggled up close to him, as close as she could get, nestled her hand between his thighs and fell asleep. Vic lay awake watching the clownish gorgon's heads on the shelves above him, their exaggerated mouths, half-expecting one of them to speak. Barbie was still there too, staring down at him with her sea-blue eyes from inside her transparent niche. With Beef's sizeable body lying across his own, there was no chance of turning off the overhead light until she woke. If one of the coin-gorgons called his name in the tiny room, it would be impossible to pretend that he hadn't heard it. He put the pillow lengthwise over his head. The television station had apparently signed off for the night, and the static came to his ears from across the hall like the relentless crash of ocean surf. He could easily have been on a seaside balcony, in the cottage he'd built with his own hands, facing east toward the Sea of Cortez. The last nail driven, the last adobe in place. After a long while, delicious waves of sleep began to sweep over Vic, but each time one did, he felt himself tumbling into air, and jerked awake.

Beef, still half in slumber, raised her head off his shoulder and mumbled. "What's happening, sweetheart?"

"It's nothing," he answered, caressing her. "I keep thinking that I'm still in the van with my head on your lap, and we're falling into one of those canyons."

She blinked, her eyes glazed and uncomprehending. "Is it over? Are we there yet?"

"No," he said. "It's not over. We're not there yet. Go back to sleep." It was going to be a long night.

It was hot already and was going to get hotter, with no shade, whirl-winds of dust and foil gum wrappers blowing, and Beef drinking coffee out of a styrofoam cup to try to get conscious. Her face was still puffy with sleep. In halter top and cutoffs, skin milky pale as a redhead's in the bright sun, she complained in a congested voice that Vic had kept waking her all night with his tossing and turning. Rows of folding metal tables made avenues in what an hour before had been a couple of vacant acres of bare dirt, with a few shovelfuls of gravel thrown down to make it look respectable. It was hard to say where all the vendors had come from, in such a small town. A few of them had out-of-state license plates—none of them expired, however.

The elderly couple next door, terminally tan, seemed to be natives. They had backed their recreational vehicle up to the selling area, so they could attach one end of a tarp to the RV for shade, and set out lawn chairs underneath. They had some kind of lathe and several engraving tools, to burn messages into the plaques of wood they were unpacking. Running a rubber tube with a nozzle on it out from the RV's kitchenette, the woman wet the earth in her immediate area with a fine spray, to keep the dust down. She and her husband had brought out a gallon thermos of lemonade, an ice chest packed with plenty of fresh fruit, and prepared themselves breakfast plates, arranging the slices of cantaloupe, watermelon, kiwi fruit and strawberries in a semi-circle so that there would still be room left to place the croissant without getting it moist. Spreading napkins over their knees to set the wicker plate holders on, they looked refreshed and well-rested. They slathered themselves with sunscreen, put on their sunglasses, donned their visors, and began to lay out merchandise on the display tables. "Great morning, isn't it?" the man called out.

"These god damned horseflies are stinging me already," said Beef.

Keith had left price tags on everything and, taking advantage of having two salespeople to man his tables at the swap meet, he'd driven over through Red Rocks Canyon to Sedona to take care of some errands. The first potential customer of the day ambled up. She was eating an ice cream cone, switching it from hand to hand because the ice cream was melting so fast. A yellowish streak had already made its way to her elbow. She fingered a cut glass bowl, eyeing the fresh smudges on it with contempt, then set it down and proceeded to perform the same operation on a pitcher.

"That's cut glass," said Vic. "You don't find many with that unusual design around these days."

"I know what it is," said the woman.

"Leave the fuckin' bowls alone unless you plan to buy one," Beef snapped.

The woman huffed, set the pitcher down, and stalked off across the grass, lobbing the remains of her soggy cone into a nearby bush. Vic took out a bottle of Windex and spritzed the sullied vessels, then wiped them clean with a paper towel. "You shouldn't run people off like that. I've got to make some money. The first customer of the day is supposed to bring good luck."

"You," she said, narrowing her eyes. "Don't mess with me." She flipped open one of the silk Japanese fans, turning her blue-veined wrist toward herself like a geisha. "I can't believe it's this hot already. Put some of that sunscreen on my shoulders, would you? They're sensitive."

Vic squirted lotion on his fingers and rubbed at her flesh. She had freckles, and a couple of moles that he hadn't noticed before. "God knows where he got this goop. It's full of sand."

"I'll probably get a rash from it. Ouch, that hurts. Go easy, do you mind?"

"It says factor fifteen. What's the highest? Three hundred? Three thousand?"

"I never can remember either. I'm probably halfway to melanoma already. Don't these crullers taste like peat moss to you?"

"They're not so bad. They probably taste funny because you haven't had your morning smoke yet."

"I was too sleepy to remember to bring my cigs along. And I still hadn't woken up enough when he pulled into the Seven Eleven to remind him to buy me another pack. I don't even know what I'm doing here. I must be out of my mind."

Vic slid a crumpled pack from his shirt pocket. "I brought them for you."

"Oh, I love you." She shook one out, lit it, and blew him a smoke ring like a kiss. "You can be pretty sweet. I even kind of liked you climbing onto me at whatever o'clock in the morning that was for a second helping. Frisky as an attack dog. That was you, wasn't it?"

"Very funny."

"Were you okay?"

"What do you mean?"

"I don't know. You seemed so agitated. Don't get me wrong; I like the body contact, but it felt like you were using me to try to spend yourself so you could settle down."

"No, it's nothing. I had a hard time getting my mind stopped."

"Still fretting over that woman?"

"That's all over. As a matter of fact, I was lying awake thinking that I don't ever want to have kids."

"Is that why you were trying to procreate with me like a billy goat? I didn't have my diaphragm in, you know."

"Oh, shit. Are you kidding?" His hand instinctively went out to touch her abdomen, as if he expected to find it full-blown.

She laughed. "It's not Jiffy Pop. Gestation doesn't work that way, I'm sorry to say. It would make women's lives a lot easier. But don't you remember when I got up to go to the bathroom again, after you practically elbowed me out of that narrow bed? I went ahead and took my diaphragm out. I was so sleepy at the time that I forgot all about it. Just this second I remembered."

"What are we going to do?"

"About what? We'll just have the baby. It might be kind of fun. We'll take him to flea markets around the country with us, and he can run and get us a hot dog from the concession stand whenever we're hungry. Won't that be nice?"

"It's just that I'm not ready to be a father."

"Relax. Don't go into testosterone shock. I'm only joking. All you have to do is say something like that, and men get so balled up about it. I told you, I'm out of practice, so I've gotten out of the habit of keeping track of whether I have the diaphragm in or out."

"Give me a drag off that cigarette."

"I didn't know you smoked."

"I don't. But I'm starting today. In the abstract, paternity sometimes sounds appealing, as long as you don't mention specific dates."

"Well, I'm past my prime childbearing years, and besides I just had my period, so you're probably in luck. The odds are about a thousand to one of my conceiving."

"Probability is starting to catch up with me. I learned that much in Oasis."

"If it happens, we deal with it. We'll get you a trophy made next door there that says World's Most Potent Male."

"My ex-girlfriend forgot to use her birth control sometimes. Not deliberately. I think in her subconscious she was halfway hoping something might accidentally happen. She didn't like for me to use anything, and for a while I'd ask her every time beforehand, to be sure she had. But I didn't want to seem like I was policing her. It kind of took the spontaneity out of things."

"You know why I think guys get so bent out of shape about this procreation business? It doesn't have anything to do with women. It's because men are all afraid they won't be good providers. That's what they fear at bottom. The caveman ethic is still alive and well. They want to be good with tools, like that engraving stuff next door there. You only pretend that your heart's desire is unbridled independence. Instead, you've spent all of human history doing mating dances, and trying to prove that an opposable thumb is good for something besides onanism."

"I don't agree. That's the opposite of the truth."

"No, I think I'm right. Men I've dated look at me like I'm a monster or something when I tell them I have no desire to raise little cretins of my own. No matter what they say, men always except a woman to get dewy-eyed when they see somebody else's baby. I'm just not into it."

The customers began to show up, in spite of the heat. Within another hour, the walkways between the tables were congested with browsers, edging around one another's sun hats. Vic found himself unaccountably shouting out to browsers as they passed, collaring them with the persistence of a panhandler, extolling the virtues of Keith's goods. Beef made no attempt to sell anything. She kept herself amused by watching him work and helping to wrap the items, make change, and enter the sales in the ledger Keith had left. Vic was on such a roll he didn't know exactly how much they'd turned over, but it was a lot. Things were moving so fast that he was starting to wonder whether he might not clear the tables before Keith returned. He would try to, anyway. When there was finally a lull, Beef smiled. "You're filled with the righteous fire this morning."

"Yeah, I might do okay at this." He rubbed his hands together. "I think I've got a knack. The gift of gab."

"The bark of bullshit."

"Come on, give me some credit. I could really get smoking if I put my mind to it. What are you smiling about? I mean I could get by. That's all I'm saying. It doesn't really matter to me whether I succeed or not, of course. I'm not in competition with anybody, okay? It's just a means to an end. I'm trying to build up a cash reserve for my new life. That casino in Oasis was my undoing."

A man had been looking over the objects on one of the tables for a few minutes, picking up this and that, without showing particular interest in any one thing. He had a beard that was meant to disguise his lack of a chin, but only pointed the fact up more. His mohawk looked as if he'd barbered himself while he was drunk and enraged, and he wore a sleeveless vest that only reached halfway around his beer belly. The pocket of the vest was decorated with metal studs.

"I'll bet you fifty dollars you can't sell anything to this Goliath," Beef whispered.

"Don't make it into a contest," he whispered back. "I'm not going to fall for that bait."

She shrugged and went back to her cigarette. "Suit yourself. If you're not up to the challenge."

"All right," he said, shaking a finger. "You're on. Just to show you that I know how to read human nature better than you. You don't know the first thing about this guy. You can't judge a book by its cover. He might be a collector and a connoissseur. Besides, I need the fifty bucks."

"Here's my fifty." She took out two twenties and a ten, and made an elaborate show of sticking them down the front of his pants.

"You'll have to trust me for my fifty. Keith said he'll pay me tonight. But remember, I can sell this guy anything. It doesn't have to be expensive."

"Fair enough."

The man picked up one of the spheroid glass insulators, pitched it into the air and caught it a couple of times, testing its weight. He hefted it above his shoulder like a shotput.

"They used to attach those to the tops of telephone poles," said Vic. "It was a crude form of containing electricity, so it didn't just shoot out anywhere and wreak havoc. Those are only a dollar apiece. You can use it for decoration. It would complement glass bricks very nicely. Art deco. Or it could be used as a doorstop or a paperweight."

The man examined the object in his grip. "Yeah, or to crush somebody's skull."

"That too. I hadn't thought of that. It would definitely inflict some damage. You must be a biker," said Vic. "Are you looking for belt buckles? We've got Harleys and Indians down at the end there. Seven apiece or three for twenty bucks."

"Who's the babe? She yours?"

"She's not merchandise. Is there something else I can help you with?"

"Don't get hot, little man. I'm just asking. I saw her fiddling with your fly there a minute ago."

"Go jerk yourself off, you slob," said Beef. "Of course, you probably can't even see your penis over that gut without using a mirror."

"Woman's got a tongue on her," said the biker. "Harsh. Tall. Seems more my size. I don't understand what she's doing with you. Why don't you come on along with me, baby?"

"The only thing the size of you is the rotunda in the Library of Congress," said Beef. "Of course you probably don't even know what that is. I doubt you've ever seen a book before. Did your mommy ever read you anything besides the Miranda Statement?"

The sellers next door were putting their trophies back in boxes, glancing over at Vic's tables and up at the heavens, as if they expected a sudden gully-washer, or a lightning bolt from an angry Zeus to strike one of their trophies. "Beef, please let me handle this. You're using unfair tactics. Let me do my job, or the bet's off." He turned back to the man. "You don't happen to be going to that biker blowout up in the Badlands, do you?"

The biker sized Vic up, considering his question. "I travel up there about every year, as a matter of fact, little man. Funny you should ask. I was just starting to think about punching you in the face, to pay you back for your woman's smart remarks, but you've piqued my interest. I haven't been able to polish up my chopper yet this week, because I'm tying up some loose ends. But I'll probably go to the Badlands for a few days."

"Well, look. I've got a proposition for you. You want to be macho, then let's talk man to man about something that really separates the men from the boys. "

"And what would that be?"

"Not tattoos and not biceps. Money. Money talks and bullshit walks. You ever hear that saying? If I give you a wholesale price on some of our belt buckles—say four dollars apiece—you could take them up to the Badlands and make a killing. Three dollars profit for you on each one, or more if you can sell them for more."

Beef flicked the ashes off her cigarette, looking from one to the other of them. "No fair. Keith said not to go down more than fifteen per cent on anything."

"This is different. I'm selling in quantity. I don't think he'll object if I cut a deal like this. You always make a smaller profit margin when you sell in volume."

"All right. Proceed."

"Now, we'd have to have cash up front, but I'll give you a receipt, and we'll refund you for any buckles you don't sell. Why don't you take a couple hundred of them up there and see what you can do? They're small, and won't take up much room on your chopper. I've got them boxed up under the table here and ready to go. What do you say?"

The man stroked his beard with both hands. "It's tempting. I'm always trying to pick up extra cash, because it takes a lot to keep that chopper tuned up right. What people don't realize is that a pretty piece of machinery like mine can suck up your money like a bottomless grease pit." He rubbed his naked belly, contemplative as the Buddha. "And on top of that, I've forked over three hundred bucks to take a correspondence course in Hotel and Motel Management, so it's tough making ends meet these days." He gave Beef a hurt look. "It's not the life of Riley, the way everybody always figures. You trash a bar, then you have to go home and study with red-rimmed eyes and a tequila hangover. Now, some of the bikers these days— the ones who aren't selling crack—try to get work in the factories. The generation before us had it easy. After the war, with the GIs and everybody so flush, it was fat city. Suburbs springing up everywhere, and the restless suburban chicks out hitchhiking in their hip huggers, itching to hop on your banana seat for a joy ride. Back then, all you had to do was bust some heads, get laid, learn a little beatnik slang to pass yourself off as a sensitive man of mystery, and try not to get the clap. Your basic Dennis Hopper stuff. But these days, with safe sex and the recession and just say no, it's slim pickings. No hitchhikers on the road except crazy old geezers that even I'm afraid to pick up."

"Amen to that," said Vic.

"You got to sweat blood before you can kick ass, put together part-time jobs here and there so you can go get stupid on your days off. I'm telling you, man, it's a bitch. I keep trying to tell my blood brothers that heavy industry is not where it's at anymore. Forget that factory shit. We're shifting over to a service economy. That's the wave of the future. Hell, even the Indians around here are starting to open casinos on their tribal lands. I figure I can get me a piece of the action, ground floor, if I can just get through this course. I'm sick of working as a bouncer and doing repo work, with no health insurance benefits. I'm getting arthritis in my hands from beating on people. So I might take you up on your offer."

"All right, then. Now you're talking."

"Except first I have to finish another piece of business I was sent over here to see about. Otherwise I don't get the bonus on this week's paycheck, with the differential for weekend work. Now it sounds to me like you're running this stand for somebody else. Didn't I hear you say Keith?"

"We're managing it," said Vic. "Why do you ask?"

"Because I'm looking for Keith Jackson. My information is that he's supposed to be out here at the swap meet today, and this is his usual spot. But he's been staying on the road a lot lately, and it's been kind of hard to track him down. He's an evasive dude."

"I'm in contact with him. Do you have a message you'd like for me to relay?"

"I sure do. Tell Keith that if he knows what's good for him, Charlie really needs to talk to him." The biker started to swagger away. Then he turned back and surveyed the tables one more time, giving them a long, hesitant, panoramic, Einsteinian look. "Yeah, and one more thing."

"You forgot the belt buckles."

"I hate to bring this up, you all have been so helpful and all, but tell Keith that if he don't come up with the money by tonight, we're going to track him down and kill his ass." From a standing position, the biker sprang so high above the table he seemed to levitate in the air, one foot slightly more aloft than the other. He looked poised to do a cosmic kick-start. Then the earth exerted a gravitational pull as strong as Jupiter's, slowing the mammoth body's upward arc, bringing it hurtling down at several times its earthly weight and g-force. Beneath his leather boots, the flimsy metal tables crumpled, and delicate fluted dishes flew into one another. Wedges of cracked glass sailed, and multicolored aggies sprayed in random directions like meteorites. Vic could hear them pinging off the side of the RV next door, and it sounded as though a few of them were rolling around in the trophies still on display.

When Keith returned, he inspected the damage to his possessions morosely, shaking his head, as if it were no more than he had expected. "Beef, I might as well not beat around the bush here. I'm in deep with a bookie. Ten thousand dollars. Off-track betting in Santa Fe. I wanted to tell you, but you can understand why I didn't. I was just going to stay around here and ride it out. But after this biker fellow coming around, I'm starting to get scared."

"Do you realize the position this puts me in?" She turned to Vic. "Keith used to be an inmate at the prison. He got nailed for buying a half gram. He was one of my parolees too, and I put my ass on the line with the trustees. I worked out the details of a contract for him to sell the handicrafts of the prison vocational program, to help him keep a steady income, so he wouldn't get into more trouble. And up until now, except for his dropping a hundred or two of his earnings now and then at the casinos, he was looking pretty good."

"Isn't there something you can do to get Charlie off my tail?"

"Just what exactly do you think I'm going to do? First off, I'm not a cop. I get them on the other end, after they've paid most of their debt to society, as you know from personal experience. Sure, you could report that you're being harassed, but the most we're likely to get at this point is a peace bond on that beer-bellied jerk who crushed your tables and mangled your merchandise. But how do you think that report's going to reflect on me, under the circumstances? Here I am working a flea market with you, when I'm supposed to be off looking for Gamma Ray."

"So in other words, Charlie has to kill me first, before he's perceived as a threat to my personal welfare."

"I'm afraid that's about the size of it. The problem is, if you report this threat to the authorities, you're going to have to tell them about your being in debt to a bookie. And that's not going to make me look so splendid either."

"No sense bringing the law into this. We're in agreement there."

"I've got a good mind to leave you here and let you pay off your debts to this man the hard way. Why is that I can never have a real vacation? I can't go off for a week or two and shack up without having you around to crawl up my ass. If they'd just slipped quietly into your house at night, and put a pillow over your head, I wouldn't have this headache right now."

Andrea came to the door wearing a man's shirt, the tails tapering off below her thighs. Her legs were bare. She seemed thinner. But maybe it was simply because he hadn't seen her for a while, and the actual dimensions of her body would assert themselves slowly after his prolonged absence. The shirt looked vaguely familiar, but he couldn't make out the true color in the frosted porch light, so there was no way to be sure about that either. Its collar was pilly, disreputable. He couldn't decide whether it would elate him or depress him if the shirt turned out to be his. It was out of character for her to wear a garment so frayed, even in the relative anonymity of sleep.

She squinted, running her hand through her hair, back along the crown of the head, the fingers with their lacquered, glossy nails spread like the teeth of a Spanish comb. When they'd lived together, she used to have her nails done every week at the Thai salon. They always looked impeccable. One time she'd persuaded him to have his done, telling him it wasn't just a woman's thing. She wanted him to look smart, finished, to enhance his natural savoir faire, as the manicurist had put it. Tilting him back in the chair, the woman had taken out the bamboo shoots and gone to work on him. He'd walked around for a week afterward with his cuticles bleeding.

"Vic. What are you doing here?" She gave a profound sigh. Even her night breath smelled sweet as clover. That was another feat of hers he'd never managed to figure out. He'd always suspected that she woke up at regular intervals during the night to pop breath mints. No one could have natural breath that fragrant all the time, especially somebody who loved curry as much as she did. The body's impurities had to come out sooner or later. He became keenly conscious of how much garlic had been in the flautas he'd eaten earlier.

"I know I promised not to come. We're passing through on the way to Baja. We need a place to crash for a few hours. Then we'll go. It's too complicated to explain."

"Who is we?"

He motioned toward the van idling on the slope of the driveway, its yellow running lights on. "Me and a couple of recent acquaintances. Say, how come they put concrete troughs across the asphalt at all the intersections? We nearly got a concussion driving over those."

"Because this is a residential neighborhood, and they don't want hellbent hoodlums ripping through here at four in the morning, waking responsible citizens out of a sound sleep."

"The driver isn't a hoodlum. But I'm afraid he's going to have an accident if we don't stop."

"I don't want to hear about it. Vic, I don't have anywhere to put three people. Can't you stay in a motel?"

"He's afraid to check into a public place. For reasons that you'd probably prefer not to know."

"So you come here instead."

"There's no danger. Humor me. You know I wouldn't be here if there was any other alternative. This guy thinks he's being followed. He's so overwrought, he's given himself an asthma attack."

"This wouldn't be the same fanatic who stole your car, would it?"

"No, a different one. All we want is to catch a few z's on your floor. If you have a couple of throw pillows, that would be plenty. Believe me, I've slept in less comfortable places recently. Tomorrow we're crossing into Mexico. Is that my shirt?"

"Why, do you want it back?"

"No, I was only curious. It looks soft and comfortable from being washed so much. Do you always sleep in it?"

"Don't start messing with my head, please. I don't know whose it is. It's the first thing I pulled out of the drawer."

"Well, whose else could it be? It looks like a man's shirt to me. Besides, you're not the kind of person who just pulls things out of drawers and throws them on."

"Would you please keep your voice down?" She stepped out onto the porch, and closed the front door behind her. "You're lucky tomorrow's Sunday, and I don't have to work."

"I thought you said summer session was over."

"Look, you might as well know that somebody's sleeping here."

"Have you already started having an affair with someone else?"

"It's not an affair. You only call it an affair if you're involved with another person at the same time. I'll tell you what. The three of you can throw down here until morning, for old times sake. Only because you say your friend's having a spell of asthma. Come daybreak, you're out of here. Consider this my last favor to you. The last. But if I hear a single crack pass your lips, I'm kicking you right back out. I know your tongue."

"And I know yours."

"It's none of your business who I'm sleeping with, or what the nature of the relationship is. You and I are no longer an item."

"Fine. It doesn't matter anyway. I brought along a woman friend myself. She's out in the van."

"You brought a girlfriend to sleep on my floor? I can't believe your chutzpah."

"Well, I wasn't going to say anything about it. But why should you mind? She and I are just good pals, like you and the mystery guest. Girl-friend is too anachronistic of a term. We're—significant others. Sym-metrical otters. It's all still indeterminate. You know how hard it is these days, with the collapse of the old semiotic systems, to know when you've definitely phased out one thing and gone onto another. First you're friends, then you're not, then you are again. Then you're lovers, then you're not, and so on. It's more semantics than anything else."

"And I suppose those hickeys on your neck are hieroglyphics."

"I have hickeys on my neck?"

"Yes, it looks like somebody's been biting you all along your neck. Don't you think you're a little old for that sort of thing? Did you give her an ID bracelet too?"

"Okay, you've made your point. So now, let's try to be adult about the situation at hand. I'm a new man, and my credo when it comes to people's personal affairs is live and let live. The four of us will get along fine, be cordial, and I won't cause you any hassles. Look, she doesn't even know you're my old girlfriend. Does this guy know about me?"

"Don't flatter yourself."

"Good. Then there's nothing to worry about. We'll both play it cool, and nobody will be the wiser. Agreed?"

"Fine with me. Why don't you tell the paranoid and your gal pal to come in. There are pillows and sheets in the hall closet. Two of you can sleep on the fold-out sofa. I don't care which two. I'm going back to bed."

The Japanese soaking tub in Andrea's back yard was set in a gazebo, behind a bamboo screen that rolled down for privacy, leaving an open-air view of a patch of ocean made even patchier by the miasma of fog that kept drifting across it, cutting off the view. Up to his neck in the scalding water of the deep cedar tub, his hair frothy with a papaya-scented spume, and clumps of it standing out from his scalp like the fronds of a palm tree, Vic relished his soak. Even the fog now seemed part of the cure, a vaporous exhalation as bracing and purgative as a Turkish bath, as it mingled with the steam condensing in the cool morning air, and the liquid-seeming crystals that dangled from the roof of the gazebo. The sweat he was working up felt wholly different in kind from the night sweats that had left mineral deposits on his skin as he lay cramped in the station wagon by the Great Salt Lake. His pores hadn't felt this unclogged in a long while. They seemed to fairly breathe underwater, amphibious and apart. Behind him now was the unrelenting geology of the Southwest, filled with fossils and petrified forests, and it was a relief to have a respite, however brief, by the seaside before he set out through still more desert country.

Vic had to be sure not to stay in this hot water too long. He was feeling giddy again, and didn't want to bring on another bout of heat exhaustion. He turned on the cold water and let it run. In the blissful silence that followed on his shutting off the tap, he could hear sea lions huskily barking in the distance. Or maybe they were symmetrical otters, yearning for asymmetry, for a release from all mammalian complications.

"Vic?"

"Yes?"

A voice came from behind the bamboo screen. "When I woke up, your friend—Beef—said you wanted to talk to me out here. I must say, she's awfully understanding. More than I would be under the circumstances."

"She doesn't know you're my—you know, ex. I told her you were just an old friend. Otherwise, I don't think she would have agreed to stop here."

"Of course she knows. I saw that as soon as we exchanged glances. She has etiquette enough to mask it, but she's not a fool."

"I hope you don't mind me using the tub."

"Have I ever begrudged you anything? Here are some towels. Listen, I hope you all will leave soon, and not hang around here all morning. I'm trying to be a sport, but the whole situation is too weird for me to deal with for very long."

"Could you please come around from behind the screen? I feel stupid talking to you this way."

"You're in the tub."

"So what? You've seen me naked before. Plenty of times. I'm down in the water, and I promise not to stand up. Besides, how else do you plan to give me those towels?" She came around the screen. She was wearing a cotton mini-dress, low-waisted and skintight, with wayfarers. "Hey, hey. Don't you think you ought to be wearing Nancy Sinatra boots with that?"

"Oh, button it."

"It looks great on you. Everything does, of course. Except that you're too thin."

"I was getting ready to say the same about you."

"How can you tell, unless you're looking where you're not supposed to be looking?"

She averted her gaze to the twirling crystals that dangled from the timbered beams of the gazebo. "I feel bloated. My stomach looks poochy to me."

"It's in your mind, Andrea."

"No, it's not. I hate it when you say that. Do I ever tell you that your insomnia is in your mind?"

"It is in my mind. That's exactly the problem."

"Well, mine is physiological. It may be that I'm about to get my period, and I'm retaining excess water, because I'm way overdue for it."

"You've been known to miss them. That happens to the hard-core athletic girls. So, am I going to get to meet your boyfriend?"

"He's not my boyfriend. He left in the middle of the night, after the circus arrived. Not that it's any business of yours, but if you have to know, I met him in a blues bar last night."

"A one-night stand, then."

"Call it what you want. I was feeling a little lonely. But don't make a big deal out of it. At least I'm not hung up on sex the way you are."

"I'm not hung up on sex."

"Yes you are. Like a fourteen year old. With you, if we missed one day for some reason, you always had to make it up on the next day, as if we were keeping score."

"I don't remember that."

"Well, I do. You don't know the pressure it created sometimes. Anyway, let's not talk about this. I came down here to apologize for being so snide last night. I feel kind of bad for doubting your good intentions, and saying I was going to throw you out. I thought you'd come here to try to sweep me off my feet again. I was mulling over our exchange, and you're absolutely right that the two of us should be able to stay good friends, and simply admit like adults the fact that a romantic relationship is never going to work out between us. There's no reason why you and I can't continue to be intimate in an innocent, platonic way. As long as we ourselves know we're in control of our emotions, know our limits, we have nothing to be ashamed of. Don't you think so?"

"Oh, yes. Absolutely."

"For instance, here we are down in this romantic setting by the sea, you don't have any clothes on, and I, your recent ex-lover, am sitting here at your side. For somebody low-minded and unsure of their own motives, it could seem inappropriate. But I don't feel embarrassed. Do you?"

"No, no. Not in the slightest. Aroused maybe, but fortunately for both of us, most of my anatomy is submerged in a tub of water right now."

"That's quite all right with me, Vic, if you're slightly turned on, as long as we don't do anything about it. I'm not offended. It gives us both a sorely needed opportunity to exercise a restraint, a mental chastity that neither of us was ever capable of when it came to each other."

"I couldn't agree more. You're taking the words right out of my mouth."

"To me, achieving that would be a kind of higher plane. Toward the end of our relationship, you couldn't stand simple caresses or gestures of tenderness. I felt I could hardly touch you, unless it was ultimately going to lead to coitus. I honestly think that's why we started getting it on so much. There was no in-between. It really became obsessive towards the end there. Here, give me that loofa. You missed a spot on your back."

"That's okay. I'll get it myself."

"No, I insist."

"You're right. Why should't you wash my back? There are parts I can't reach."

He gave himself over to her casual ministrations, the loofa's touch as wholesome and rough as the chapped hands of a kindly, ruddy-faced laundress. He might as well have been sitting in a split hogshead barrel with a cork stopping the bunghole, being rubbed down with lye soap on a Saturday night while his kinfolk gathered around to wait their turn.

"But I don't want to lay it all on you. I'm as much to blame as you are. No question." She had dropped the loofa, and was slowly, absently massaging the suds on his scalp. "Even after I left, and moved down here, I fantasized about you. Did you ever fantasize about me?"

"Uh, yeah. Whew. Once in a while. I can't remember specific dates. Could you turn that cold tap back on? The temperature in here is still too high."

"Of course. My pleasure. You've got the thickest, cowlickest hair I've ever seen on a man. The fragrance of your locks smells heavenly. Almost as if you had a floral wreath around your head. Like Narcissus, or one of those Greek demigods who used to drive the wood nymphs wild. But I realized, especially after our conversation on the phone, what a foolish and self-destructive indulgence that was. If you'd come here a couple of days ago— by yourself, that is—we probably would have ended up jumping right into bed together, as usual, to try to solve our problems. Even last night, I was wavering a little, out of habit. But after my one-night stand, I realized I need to be on my own for awhile, out of a relationship. I'm glad you gave me enough time to think things through. Thanks for not insisting. This way, we can have a healthier and more mature human intercourse. No mind games."

He grabbed her wrist, the one she was washing him with, and pulled her down toward him. "Let's be immature, just once more. Let's have the old kind of intercourse. Then we can behave like responsible people. I promise not to regress."

"Vic, stop it. You're going to get the front of my dress completely soaked, and then we really will have a lot of explaining to do."

"Please. I'm not kidding. I'm on fire right now. I'm ready to trade a few minutes of passion for a lifetime of repentance. Let me take you in my arms. I'm going to go crazy if I can't feel your body against mine. As much as we've made love, what does one encounter more or less mean?"

"Don't beg. You don't mean it. And you have somebody else waiting for you up at the house." She shook off his grip with her wrist. "We're getting along so well, having such a pleasant, productive conversation, and you have to spoil it. In spite of all the fog, we're not on the moors, so don't start acting like Heathcliff."

"I see how it is. Touché. You've paid me back with interest."

"I have no idea what you're talking about. Tilt your head back, please. I can't get to you otherwise."

"You seem to be getting to me just fine." Vic closed his eyes, breathed through his nose, and let the polished, flawless edges of her manicured nails scratch softly against his scalp. She was saying something to him, something sensible and temperate, possibly even sincere, but his ears had begun beating and he couldn't hear. She seemed to be speaking underwater, and the beating was like the throb of a sump pump laboring desperately to empty all the liquid so he could understand her correctly. *All right, Vic. Have your way with me. But on one condition. I want us to flow together in a sensory deprivation tank. Immobile, silent, lying together without speaking, suspended in the medium. No words to get in the way. Buoyant and effortless. No clothes to remove, or diaphragms to put in, or awkward limbs to figure out what to do with. No post-coital tristesse. Weightless, without gravity. The boundaries of our bodies dissolving into the water and into each other.* Lather slid down his neck onto his shoulders, and she streaked it across them with the soft skin of her fingertips. "Your shoulders are still muscular, even though you're thinner. Are they tight from all the driving? Or have you been tearing trees out of the ground by the roots, like Heathcliff?"

"I haven't torn out any yet. But I might before the day is over."

She massaged his shoulders, working her way under his armpits around to his chest, and her lips grazed the flesh of his earlobe. You smell sweet, she said. I could drink you up. Then drink me, he said. Drink me to the lees. I'm poison, not an antidote, but let us both become corpses, lost souls, damnéd together for all eternity, if that's to be the price of our transgression. I don't care, she answered. I want to die la petite mort. She was kissing the back of his neck, his upper arms, strands of her hair sliding across his skin. When she arched her back and perched one knee on the edge of the tub, he turned and pulled her into the water, into his waiting arms. She slid without effort, settling into the depths of the bath with the weightless ease of a mermaid, one who turns out to have the blissful lower half of a human woman. He discovered that magical fact of metamorphosis by putting his hands around her buttocks and looking down to admire the newfound limbs flashing beneath the surface ripples. Water had soaked through her mini-dress, and it clung to her slender form, showing the dark, hard, shrunken nipples. She seemed lighter than ever before, her figure girlish, almost boyish, a pure, distilled essence of the Andrea he had known. She swirled easily, so that her back was to him, and snuggled the soft curve of her bottom between his legs. Satan, get thee behind me, she said. The air above them had turned dense as the heavens with the exhalations of their desire.

The very waters roiled. They pressed their drenched bodies together, panting and humid. Now I know what they mean by steamy, said Vic.

Let's make love, my darling. I'm as trembling and fragile as a hothouse violet. Right here? But—what about the others?

Yes, right here. I don't care what happens. Let the devil take the hindmost, and in this case that means you. Help me take my clothes off before I start thinking about all the complications, and change my mind. She loosened the elastic band of her ponytail, and shook her mane. But if we're going to betray them, I want to be ravished with my taffy-colored tresses spilling over my shoulders. I only wish they were as raven as my black heart.

Surf pounded the craggy coast, flinging flecks of foam so far that they nearly reached the spot of their tryst. Wraiths of fog swirled among the stone deities littered about the yard. Vic struggled to peel the saturated dress, tighter than a laced bodice, from Andrea's heaving bosom. The weight of the cotton folds, running with rivulets of water, made it difficult to pull the dress over her shoulders, but she gripped the outer sides of the tub, and after two or three tries he managed to force the collar over her now impossibly tangled mane of hair.

Take me, you sinful satyr, she whispered. Take me now, short and sharp and goatish. Their bodies fell together and she rained kisses on the blond fleece of his chest. Because she was shorter than he, he tried bending his legs, then kneeling, but either way, he couldn't seem to achieve the proper height for entering her. He was either too high or too low. Too low, or too high.

Wait a minute.

Oh darling.

If I could just—the sides of this tub are slippery with soap scum.

I feel so warm and yielding.

Could you try sitting on that ledge? There's a little short ledge there, about halfway down. Right there.

Vic, the magic moment is passing. I want this encounter to be spontaneous. It's my wicked fantasy.

I know. As soon as you can—sit—okay, I think this is going to work.

I keep slipping off. The seat's too slick and narrow. Oh, I don't think this is such a good idea. This is the way I always felt when you started haranguing me about my diaphragm.

"Are you listening to what I'm saying?"

"What? Sorry. I lost my head for a minute." He looked her up and down. Her hair was perfectly coiffed, and her dress bone dry, dry as dust, dry as the inside of Vic's mouth.

"Okay, I'm stepping out now. Avert your gaze and hand me one of those towels."

"Now who's being prudish? Well, well, there's a familiar sight."

"Cut it out. Don't look. Don't start anything I can't finish." Vic quickly wrapped the towel around himself and sat on the gazebo's wooden bench. His skin was smoking like a block of dry ice. It was the kind of ice that slivers are chipped from and dropped into beakers in grade B horror flicks, to create newer and more perfect life forms from the defective ones that fell short on the first go-around.

"Now, what is it you called me down here to talk to me about?"

He panted. "Christ, I'm thirsty. I want you to go to Mexico with us."

"Are you out of your mind? You've got your nerve, buddy."

"No, please, just hear me out. You said you had a couple of weeks break before you started back to classes, right?"

"I'm listening. Impatiently."

"The thing is, I need you to help me recover the stolen car. This guy who took it, we're pretty sure we know where he's going, because of the deed he gave me."

"You mean coupon."

"If he abandons the car, or if they catch him and impound it, I might not be able to get it back without you there to claim it."

"I told you before, I don't have anything to do with that car anymore. It's yours."

"Actually, Andrea, it's still yours. Legally, I mean."

"What? I *told* you to change the registration into your name, because I didn't want to pay for all the parking tickets you were bound to pile up. You didn't do what I asked?"

"I meant to. I didn't have the twenty dollars at the time for the fee to switch the title over. Then I sort of forgot about it."

"You bastard. You *bastard*. Then you'll just have to get along without wheels. Wait a minute. You didn't do something stupid like leaving marijuana in it, did you?"

"No, no. Nothing like that. But all of my journals are in there, plus the stories I wrote. And the letters from you, and the notes you used to leave me around the house. All the important stuff. That's mostly what I was taking with me to New York."

Now her gaze really was averted. She thwacked a towel against a wooden post. "You don't quit, do you?"

"All I need is for you to come along for a few days, four or five tops. I'm certain the car will be down there. And I really do promise to behave. I won't do anything to make you feel uncomfortable."

"I can't believe this is happening. What about your friends?"

"I expect Keith to part company with us once we get down into Mexico. And as for Beef, well, it's just kind of up in the air. I only met her a couple of days ago. She's mainly going down to try to find this prisoner. She's a professional. She'll understand the arrangement, if I'm honest, and I tell her the real reason you're going down, which is that you're the owner of the station wagon."

Andrea shivered, like someone about to be taken with a sudden flu. "Go get dressed, Vic. Before you catch a chill."

After they'd carried the luggage outside and loaded it in the van, Andrea removed the tarp from her convertible in a single snapping gesture. The MG shone red as a fresh coat of lipstick. The dashboard console was made of wood—the console of a pleasure craft. There was barely enough room behind the front seats for anything more than a couple of tennis rackets and an overnight bag. The car was made for tooling about with your main squeeze in resort areas, the surfaces of their roads as meticulously maintained as their golf courses.

"Where did you get this? They must be paying you pretty well at your new job if you can afford this kind of wheels."

"It's my father's. I only have it on loan."

"It's not made for the roads of Baja, from what I hear about them," said Beef.

"I'm aware of that. But as Vic mentioned, I'll be coming back before the rest of you will, so I need to drive separately."

Beef shrugged, slid shut the side door to Keith's van and turned to Vic. "Go ahead and ride with Andrea," she said quietly. "I'm not going to do the jealousy thing. I'm too old for that. Just remember who you came here with."

Keith's van pulled away from the curb and the MG, with Andrea at the wheel, fell in behind. The fog had lifted, leaving a crystalline day in its wake, the air so clear that funnels of breeze made the windglass squeak. The air currents playfully tousled Vic's hair, like the fingers of a fond uncle. The weather was almost too perfect to be believed.

The college kids down in Ensenada were partying hearty. A Jeep with a roll bar and oversized knobby tires maneuvered past the automobiles double-parked on the congested street. The Jeep's driver sat high above the local traffic. Hair moussed, smoked wraparound sunglasses strapped to his face, and sleeves ripped out of his workshirt, he drove with one hand, and in the other held a beer can encased in a styrofoam holder. Bearing down on the steering wheel to flex his triceps, he had the cocksure manner of a prom king gazing down on his subjects from a parade float. His radio was turned up full blast, so he could treat outdoor bystanders to a constant thumping bass line and cri de couer, the rock falsetto magnified by the painful distortions of undersized woofers and tweeters. It was only late morning, but a happy hour atmosphere prevailed. Tourists wandered along the sidewalks from bar to bar with the smiling alacrity of mariachis. Their festive mood as they spilled from doorways didn't seem dampened in the least by the dumptrucks, or the flatbeds piled high with sacks of mortar, or the cement mixers that rumbled past, shaking the foundation of a street narrow as an alley, and creating a haze of lime dust and diesel exhaust that made Vic's eyes smart.

Two young Indian women with smooth faces leaned against the boarded facade of a construction site. The women had taken time out from selling woven ankle bracelets to watch the boozy pilgrimage with the patient, clinical intensity of anthropologists. A child rode on the hip of each, bolstered by a cloth sling, and the women chatted without ever looking at one another or taking their eyes off the tourists across the street from them. Once in a while one or the other would hold up one of the various coat hangers they had draped with ankle bracelets woven in multicolored yarn. But they didn't seem to be trying very hard to sell their goods. From the looks of it, they had already covered the immediate territory with pretty good success. Most of the tourists had bracelets banded to their ankles, as if they were roosters and pullets tagged for an agricultural experiment in mate selection and breeding.

A teenage girl with sun-streaked hair bumped into Vic while trying to squeeze past him on the narrow sidewalk, and spilled some of her margarita onto his shirt from her go-cup. "Oops! Sorry about that," she laughed, stumbling off the curb and onto the uneven bricks of the street, casually confident that her natural charms and cultivated throatiness were sufficient to extricate her from all possible run-ins and embarrassments with the opposite sex. She was smashed, and the glassy golden wafers of her pupils couldn't get a very good fix on him, but her instincts kept her asking plausible questions. "Are you with the ASU group or the SDSU group?"

"Neither," said Vic. "I'm with the control group." He wanted to be as drunk and shitfaced carefree as her, and had been working diligently for the past hour or so at achieving that enviable state, ordering one frozen margarita after another, but without much palpable success so far. As his three companions made casually strained conversation over lunch, he'd excused himself to take a breather. Everybody had always told him how potent the drinks were down here, how mixer was expensive and tequila cheap, so the bartenders gave you triple shots to save money, but he felt like he'd been eating sno-cones. The first couple had tasted pretty good, but there were only so many sno-cones you could scarf down before you ended up with an ice cream headache.

There had been a brief holdup at the border crossing, while the *guardias* held a discussion among themselves about what exactly Keith's various inhalers were for. To Keith's credit, he'd handled the situation with a surprising cool. In his mangled but relaxed Spanish, he made small talk with the *guardias*. He'd been back and forth across to the border towns so often, buying wares for his flea market stand, that the control post seemed no more threatening to him than a toll booth. He just wanted to take his friends down for some of those good seafood tacos in Ensenada, he'd told them. He had a hankering. The *guardias* nodded, comprehendingly. They loved seafood tacos too. They waved the van through.

Strangely, they hadn't given more than a glance at the rifle mounted in Keith's van. They apparently believed in the right to bear arms, and when Vic asked about this, Keith told him that lots of hunters came down to Baja. It abounded in both small and large game and that was one of the things that attracted so many weekend hunters from California. For somebody who had never been south of Ensenada, he certainly seemed to know an awful lot about it.

Even though Vic hadn't succeeded in getting drunk, and was in fact more sober than when he started, the ice cream headache was starting to ebb as he stood on the sidewalk watching the college kids cavort. Or perhaps it was just diffusing itself throughout his body, settling itself into a low-grade existential ache, as yellowish-green as a glass of barium sulfate. He felt transparent, a visible man, the opacity of his convoluted innards there for all to see, if they cared to look. He was tied in knots. He handed his empty fluted souvenir glass to a passing collegian, a wandering Greek with Zetas and Deltas emblazoned on his chest and deltoids. The Greek, reeking of bottled wisdom, had abundant ringlets of sandy hair and his physique was as perfect as Michelangelo's David. Feeling a sudden blind onrush of *agape*, and nothing to affix it to, Vic squeezed the youth's arm, told him to keep the glass. As he wandered back into the restaurant to rejoin his companions, he heard the fraternity boy say "What in the fuck is wrong with that dude? He's like palmin' me like I'm his fuckin' homeboy or something. I hate that shit."

"Fuck it," said another voice. "The dude is just polluted."

That night, they stayed in a hotel south of Ensenada. Vic awoke early, after having gone to bed late, to find Beef lying across from him in bed, eyes open. He'd managed little more than a catnap.

"You don't mind that I invited Andrea along, do you? The car is in her name."

"I already told you it's fine. Just don't keep bringing it up. It's not like we're married."

They started to make love. There was a creaking in the corridor, and she sat bolt upright, as if she expected the desk clerk to come storming in with her passkey like a fire-eating housemother, to expose their shameful and licentious wallowing, to demand to see their marriage license. The clerk already had their passports in her possession, locked in a safe behind the front desk, as supposedly required by some federal tourist statute, and she knew their last names were different. When they failed to produce a marriage license, she would inform them that they had violated several of the conjugal laws of the constitution of the Republic of Mexico by illegally fornicating and committing acts of fellatio out of wedlock in a public hotel.

After their frantic coupling, they hastily threw on their bathing clothes, foregoing any feeble afterglow that might have ensued had they chosen to take the risk of lying entangled on the bed for a few more moments. Down at the hotel pool, prostrate as Holy Week penitents on their chaise lounges, they tried their best not to look like people who'd rushed downstairs into the scorching, lidless eye of the Mexican sun after a bout of lovemaking.

A middle-aged couple from Oaxaca who spoke English, the only other persons at the pool, engaged them in conversation. "Ah, yes," remarked the Oaxacan man, smearing tropical oil on his deep, grizzled chest. "We noticed you coming in last night. We share the same floor, I believe. Small world, isn't it?"

"Do you have children, then?" the wife wanted to know. "Are they up in the room, or did you leave them with the grandparents so you could get away for a few days and make another baby?" The man leered chummily in Vic's general direction. "Let's see some pictures," demanded the woman, her smile as relentless as the sun from beneath the bill of her neon visor, her cleavage yawning, a copper canyon of licit fecundity, as she turned toward them on the chaise lounge with an outstretched, expectant hand. "No pictures," said Beef. "We don't have any children."

"You don't? I have seven kids and five grandkids already, and I'm only fifty." She and her husband, who was so virile his eyebrows needed trimming, both gave the American woman hooded looks of mute sympathy.

They then glanced over at Vic, who had deposited his body in the furthermost chaise lounge in the row. He remained horizontal, motionless and silent behind mirrored sunglasses, holding a novel stiff-armed above his face, while he read the same paragraph over and over. The Mexican couple lowered their voices a decibel or two to a mild shout. They were modern; they knew it wasn't always the woman's fault, like everyone used to believe back in the old, superstitious days when they stoned women for that sort of thing. There was always the possibililty of a low sperm count—sperm, was that how you said it? the woman wanted to know. She couldn't help adding an *e* at the beginning, *esperm*, *esperm*, it was a hard word to say for a native speaker of Spanish.

"Excuse me," said Vic, "I'm breaking out in hives. I'd better get out of the sun for a few minutes." He set down his book and wandered out of the pool area, over into the courtyard. One of the chambermaids, holding a long-handled stick, approached a fig tree planted among the date palms, as if about to perform an oblation. Standing beneath the fig tree, she reached high up into the branches with the wooden pole, and knocked down a single one of the green-skinned figs. Gathering it from the ground, she stripped the skin and chewed each shred of the fruit with the utmost parsimony.

He meandered down to the deck behind the hotel. The white sand of the hotel beach had already been raked, assiduously picked clean of litter, and planted with neat rows of oversized umbrellas. Andrea came jogging up the sand, on her way back from what was apparently a long, arduous run on the beach. She wore a heavy, impermeable rubber vest and had leg weights attached to her ankles with velcro strips. The skin of her face looked glassy, drawn and hard. Walking about in a circle to cool down, she was as quivery and lathery with sweat as a thoroughbred after a difficult race. She'd always been hard-core about her running. She had incredible self-discipline. When she was on a jag, she never missed a day, not even when she had the flu. Andrea believed that if you elevated your body temperature enough, you would, in her phrase, ream out the sickness. Her body, and her affection for Vic, were the only real fanaticisms that she had allowed herself during the time they were together. And one of those two passions, anyway, seemed to have remained intact.

"Hi. I can't believe you've already been out for a run. It's just now daybreak."

"I've been up for hours. You know I've always taken my fitness seriously."

"Next time you plan to go out early, knock on my door and I'll join you."

She gave his arm a sisterly pat and started up the stairs. "I'm sure you have your own ways of staying in shape."

"You're not trying to lose weight, are you? You don't need to be any thinner. I've never seen you so lean in my life."

"I'm just trying to maintain." She turned back. "Vic?"

"What is it?"

"Nothing. Never mind. Let's just get where we're going as efficiently as we can, okay? I don't consider this a vacation. I want to be home in two days."

    The two vehicles crawled in tandem along a recess in the earth that was probably a creek bed long since run dry. The party was lost. The backroad they'd originally been on was criscrossed by dozens of dirt trails bounded by slashes of reed grass, tentacles of thistles, and yellow sunflowers with centers black as burnt paper. All of the trails were gouged by ancient tire tracks, none of them were marked, and no buildings appeared anywhere in sight along the horizon by which to orient oneself. Once, they'd come across a ramshackle corral, constructed out of decayed cardon ribs, the hardwood dry-warped, bowed and irregular. From within, a single listless and skeletal cow watched them. The corral was trampled down at one end, the result of some moment of animal fury long since spent. The cow could easily have walked out of the corral at that end, but there was nowhere else to go anyway, so it remained, keeping up appearances.

    After fruitless searching for a hospitable campsite, the party hadn't been able to relocate the original road they'd branched off from. The going remained slow because the MG had to navigate around rock piles and ease past rut after rut breaking over the chassis like petrified sea waves. The van, too, jounced and jounced, leaning heavily to one side or the other with its superfluous cargo. When they reached the creek bed, Vic suggested that they drive in it, reasoning that populations tended to build their dwellings as close to water as possible, and perhaps this creek actually ran at certain times of year. Not having any better arguments to offer, the rest agreed. The creek bed gradually widened, and the flat terrain gave way to hummocks and hillocks of irregular shapes. The walls of a ravine rose up sharply on either side, leading to open cliff and stone shelf. Wild fig trees with white bark on the trunks and branches grew straight out of the cliffsides. The trees, wizened as licorice, had established their roots on bare rock, working the filaments into the most minute cracks, leeching out minerals to nourish the shrivelled figs. The roots were the same white color as the tree, and from a distance looked like water that had frozen as it poured over the boulders of the arroyo. The dried branches of the dead fig trees that had lost their grip and fallen down into the ravine were so porous and weak that they probably wouldn't make a very good campfire if the party had to end up pitching camp in the creek bed.

Striated cardon cacti loomed, vertical and totemic, growing out of patches of thin topsoil on the floor of the ravine. The landscape didn't appear to have changed much in the previous million years. Vic was starting to feel drowsy from the monotonous heat, but the jolting kept him awake. All at once Andrea punched the MG's accelerator. Its engine sputtered to life. As if she were on the Southern California freeway, she pulled alongside the van, signalling with flashing headlights that she wanted to pass. Keith tried to maneuver his van to one side, to let the MG by, but the channel was too narrow. The MG ran up the embankment, crazily as a bumper car in a carnival ride, and for a motionless second seemed sure to overturn. Then, darting back down into the channel like a desert lizard running for cover from a hawk, it overtook the van, running roughshod through troughs and over rocks until the air was filled with a dry, sharp report that stopped the MG in its tracks.

"It's the rear axle," said the mechanic. "You wouldn't believe how many axles and transmissions I fix in the course of a year. I don't know why you people insist on bringing this kind of car down here. It's not fit for the territory. This isn't Tijuana. You're lucky we had a tow truck on hand to haul it out of there. Had to get us one on account of all the weekend wilderness warriors touring in their sedans."

"It's my father's car, and I have to get back up North as soon as possible. Can you fix it?"

"Oh, I can fix it. As for the exterior, the whole right side is caved in. I can hammer it back into shape, more or less, but you'll have to go to a real body shop to get it restored proper. Folks around here, those lucky enough to have a car, just want to know that the thing runs. But I know how particular Angelenos are about their automobiles, souping them up and waxing them every couple of days."

"I'm not an Angeleno."

"As for the axle, I can rig something. I doubt I'll be able to round up one for this precise make and model, but I've got all kinds of wrecked cars back there in the junkheap, from tourists like you who came down this way over the years and decided it was less trouble to just abandon their vehicles. If I can't get a close matchup for your wheelbase, I'll machine the axle down to where it will fit."

The repair shop was a quonset hut of corrugated tin smack in the middle of nowhere. Engine parts littered the makeshift plank shelves in no particular order—carburetors, corroded spark plugs, yellowing cardboard boxes containing superannuated fuel filters as brittle as stale tortillas. An oak beam got from somewhere or other ran across the center of the ceiling. At one end of it, a hulking rusted red engine hung suspended like a carcass in a smokehouse from a huge hook screwed into the beam.

"Ain't that a Cessna?" Keith asked.

The mechanic nodded. "Sure is. The pilot of a light aircraft had to make a crash landing hereabouts a few years ago, and bent the struts on his plane. The engine caught fire and they put it out with sand. He left it here, saying he'd come back for it, but he never did. That's how I get most of my supplies. Must have been one of those rich Angelenos who had two or three more in the hangar at home. Pilots hired by the weekend hunters come over here from Bahía once in a while to salvage some part or other off it. They all know where to find me."

"You'll make it fit?" Andrea asked. "I don't know that much about cars, I admit, but an axle isn't something you guess about. If it happens to fall off while I'm driving, it's not as though I'll be in much shape to come back and ask for a refund."

The mechanic sipped a Coke, in no seeming hurry to reply. He set the bottle, its glass white with scratches, down on the counter and studied the level of fluid in it for a moment or two. "No sense getting frustrated with me, little lady. I'm not the one who was drag racing in the creek bed. I said I'll fix it and I'll fix it. I'm honest, and I know my business."

Andrea glared at Vic. "You're a jinx on my cars. Cosmically speaking, this is your fault, and you're going to pay me back every penny. So you'd better start sending out job applications. How much is this going to cost me?"

"Fifty dollars for the tow, and let's see, depending on whether I have to machine the axle or not, I estimate about five hundred for parts and labor, plus another hundred to hammer those dents out. So, six fifty U.S., all together."

Andrea gave a fatalistic sigh, took out her American Express card, and slapped it on the counter. "I'll be back to get the MG in a couple of days," she said.

"This will take me at least a week. And we don't take credit cards," said the mechanic.

The kayakers had dragged their boats ashore and left them sitting in a row on the shoreline's variegated pebbles. Having already set up a makeshift camp, Vic and the others watched them arrive in the dusk. The fiberglass sea kayaks, low and tapered, bright as war paint, ochre and crimson, looked like the dugouts of a savage tribe. Windburned and decked out in gaudy garments of goretex and polypropylene, layer upon waterproof layer, the kayakers had the lean, ruthless, desperate look of foragers disembarking in a land of draught after a long and thirsty voyage. But they turned out to be friendly. They asked if they could throw their sleeping mats down alongside the party already there, and offered to exchange some of the fish and clams they had caught that day for a couple of cold brewskis. Everyone set to work wrapping potatos in foil, opening cans of sauce, popping the tops off bottles of beer with a Swiss army knife. Soon a fish stew was burbling away in a battered, carbon-blackened aluminum kettle perched atop a makeshift grill of sticks, that had to be repaired every few minutes with new sticks as the old ones burned away.

The wind was high, sending embers dancing wildly aloft, blowing streaks of cloud and bluish smoke across the moon. No one could decide for sure whether the moon was full or not, but it hung low on the horizon, low as only a desert moon can be. The air had turned chilly enough for cotton sweaters and windbreakers, which got handed out indiscriminately. Beef put on Vic's cardigan, one he had been dragging around with him for years.

Everything tasted good, even the canned sardines in tomato sauce, which got passed around as finger food after the fresh fish had been consumed. Beef made a show of throwing her head back and eating them whole, as if she were swallowing goldfish. An occasional strong gust rippled jackets, and sent laughter and wisps of conversation out over the water. An easy cameraderie had set in. Andrea, who had been looking visibly queasy all day, sat close to the ashy driftwood campfire that had been built up in reckless tiers, and was now exhaling its hot breath on the assembled company, like a gregarious and wanton drunk at a party. She huddled herself as if chilled, crosslegged, staring into the flames, shadows licking across her gaunt face.

The four kayakers said they were part of a scientific group staying on an island a few miles offshore. The team had been cataloguing mollusks and studying tidal pools for the past two weeks. There were a lot of varieties of clams and such in this area. The four of them had been sent ashore to travel into town the next day and replenish some of the group's supplies. Beef wanted to know whether they thought it might rain tonight. She'd noticed that they hadn't brought any tents along with them from the island, and she said that they, too, were going to be sleeping under the stars, not having brought along all the proper camping equipment.

"Rain? Doubtful," said one of the unshaven kayakers, chewing a dried apricot with his mouth open. "Once in a blue moon it really pours, but in this ecosystem you average about an inch a year."

"I think the whole continent is averaging about an inch this year," said Vic. "I heard some thunder claps over the Rockies a few days ago, just east of the Great Salt Lake, but no rain fell, and I haven't seen a single drop hit the ground between here and there."

"Water levels are definitely down," said another kayaker. "The tides around here have receded from the previous time we stayed on the island. A lot of the tidal pools aren't where they used to be, and even the salinity of the seawater is greater. When you're swimming, you can feel it buoy you up. It's kind of a weird year, weather-wise."

After they'd all drunk a couple more beers, Andrea set a can of cold water on the campfire to boil for tea. She was obviously still sick to her stomach about her father's MG. She'd even thrown up in Keith's van, what with all the jolting earlier in the day. The kayakers, who had a way of elbowing one another just for the fun of it, gave each other significant frisky looks, and finally one of them said "Hey, we really appreciate you guys popping a few frosty ones for us. Since we have to haul all our own drinking water over there to the island, the jefe doesn't let us pack in beer too, because it's a waste of space. Anyway, if you're into it, we'd like to show a *tokin'* of our appreciation, if you catch my drift. We've got some dynamite buds. I can roll up a couple of J's right now. This stuff will knock you on your can. I mean, if you're not into it, the four of us can just blow a couple among ourselves, but you're welcome to *joint* in." His eyebrows wiggled.

"How did you get marijuana across the border? Or did you buy it down here?"

"Got to know the trade routes, bro'. The big advantage of coming down the Pacific coast in a sea kayak as opposed to a car is that there's no border crossing." He removed a zippered rubber pouch from inside his clothing. "I don't like buying grass in a foreign country from people I don't know, with all the narcs around these days, so I pack along my own. The equipment trucks of the jefe met us in El Rosarito, and trucked our kayaks overland. This," he said, licking the adhesive edge of a Zig-Zag, "is one of the sweet little perks of braving the open sea instead of coming down the easy way." He nimbly handrolled a cigarette in the rice paper. Its contours were as perfect and streamlined as those of his docked kayak. "This torpedo will definitely sink your boat."

"Sounds good to me," said Beef, smiling as she stretched a hand out to receive the proffered cigarette. "Since we'll be getting to Bahía tomorrow, this could be our last night of pleasure." The rice paper burned down erratic and fast as she took a soulful toke. Moistening the tip of her finger, she anointed the jagged, blackened edge with saliva.

"Ditto," said Keith. "I haven't had any decent weed in I don't know how long."

A long, translucent curtain of smoke drifted out of Beef's mouth. "I don't think you ought to be smoking any of this, Keith," she said, her tone of voice perfunctory and a little dreamy.

"Oh, I see. So everybody else is going to cop a nice buzz, and I'm just supposed to sit around by my lonesome and get a contact high."

"Well, whatever," said Beef, her eyes mischievous. She stood up, for no particular reason, and stretched her body languidly. The kayakers looked at her hungrily, eyes glinting, as if they'd been marooned on their island without women, and had returned to the mainland after two years instead of two weeks. From the way they were shifting their legs around on the pebbles, Vic felt sure they were trying to make sure their boners didn't show. "Come over here, Keith, and I'll give you a proper shotgun. I'm going to blow you away, desperado."

Keith leaned over until his face was almost touching hers. She flicked the ashes from the cigarette and inserted the glowing ember into her mouth. Keith opened his mouth, his body came close to hers, and he slid his parted lips along the shaft until they met hers. She put her arms around him. The joint was hidden beyond the inky concavities of their faces. Keeping her eyes open and looking directly into Keith's, she blew a long, languorous snake of smoke into him, so much that trailers of it came issuing out of his nostrils. He broke out in a sweat. His eyes rolled back in his head, leaving only the whites to shine in the light of the campfire. After a long, motionless pause they disengaged. He exhaled slowly, savoring the smoke again as it left his body. "Thanks, Beef," he said. "That felt good. It's been a long while. I forgot how sweet it is."

"Anytime," she answered.

Each time the first joint came around to him, and the second one, and the third one, Vic took a puff. He was determined to get high. He realized that Beef was hardly aware of his presence. She was playing some ridiculous hand game with one of the kayakers, monotonous and childish, but it seemed to reduce both of them to laughter each time they locked pinkies. Andrea had retreated into herself, giving him monosyllabic answers when he tried to talk to her. The moon had gone definitively behind cloud cover. The metal can sat lopsided on the charred grate of sticks. Everyone had fallen silent, sated, stoned. The kayakers were passing around a bottle of tequila that had been produced from somewhere. With nobody remembering to tend to the campfire, it had died down to sporadic runnels of flame. Keith had been smoking with the greatest enthusiasm, even bogarting, but now he too had a slightly uncomfortable expression on his face, like somebody who's just eaten the worm in the tequila. Vic closed his eyes and lay flat on his back against the smooth pebbles. Finally, he had a buzz on. He was stoned out of his gourd. The world was spinning like a playground beneath a dizzy child.

The sound of Keith's wheezing broke the stillness. Now Keith was retching, coughing up sputum, and walking about with one hand pressing against his chest. The way his hand bore down, he looked as if he was trying to shatter his breastbone. He kept shaking his head miserably, attempting to say something, and finally he managed to blurt out "Oh God, Vic. I think I really fucked myself this time."

"Why did you smoke in the first place? And you, Beef, why in the fuck did you egg him on? You couldn't leave well enought alone, could you?"

The kayakers stood around uncomfortably, trying to get their shit together. None of them knew CPR, they said, but they had a snakebite kit in one of the kayaks, if that was any help. "No," said Vic, "he just needs his inhaler."

He hastened to the van. Vic rummaged around on the dashboard in the dark and found an inhaler. As he hurried back to where Keith was now lying, his eye alighted on the metal can of boiled water sitting lopsided on the charred grate. His hand seized it. When he tried to jerk his hand back, the can stuck to it like dry ice, and a strip of skin from his palm shredded off, the way a plastic bag does when it hits hot metal. Trying to ignore the stinging sear, he wrapped somebody's discarded sweater around it and held the can to Keith's lips.

"Here."

Keith took a drink, spat and retched again. "Too hot."

"I said drink it."

"I want to. But it's. Going to. Scald my throat."

"I don't care. You should have thought of that before."

Keith was crying, or maybe there were tears in his eyes from the strain of coughing.

Vic laid the can down on the ground and took a deep breath. "I'm really sorry, Keith. I don't know why I did that. Here's your inhaler. Do you want me to shake it for you?"

"No. Just hand it here, please."

"Here you go."

When his coughing was under control, they situated him comfortably in his sleeping bag. Keith seemed humiliated by the episode. He lay rigid with his eyes closed. Beef, who said she would stay next to him, stroked his hair and gave Vic a sharp, reproving look. Vic wandered away from the campsite to take a walk down the deserted shoreline. Since there was so much cloud cover, he at least needed a point of reference so he wouldn't get lost too easily. He wanted to get away, but he also wanted to be able to retrace his path. He stuck his hand in the sea water, and let it bathe the wound on his hand. It stung, but little by little, the sting dulled. Walking alongside the wash of waves sluicing through the pebbles, he detected a faint sound above the white noise. When he turned around, Andrea stood directly behind him. "You scared me. You shouldn't sneak up on a person like that. How long have you been following me?"

"A while." Her hair was down loose, and the gusts off the Sea of Cortez had tangled it. She phosphoresced. Her skin was so transparent and her flesh so spare, he could hear the wind singing in the interstices between her bones, making them tinkle like wind chimes.

"We need to talk," she said.

"About what?" Foam licked about his legs, saturating the cuffs of his trousers.

"I'd made up my mind not to tell you at all, because I don't want to get you all upset over nothing. I've already thought the matter over, and decided the proper course of action. But I figured you were within your rights to know. So I'm discharging my duty. Consider this a simple notification."

"Notification of what? You make it sound like a legal summons."

She laughed grimly. "It's perverse. The way the fates work, it probably happened that day when we were packing to move to the new place, and having all those arguments. The day Gorby ran away. I tested twice, because I wanted to be sure. It came out blue both times."

"You're pregnant?"

"I want to assure you right away that I didn't forget to put in my diaphragm. I know that's the first thing that will leap to your mind. But I didn't get this way on purpose, so don't start blaming me."

"You're pregnant?"

"As soon as I get back to San Diego, I'll take care of it. There's plenty of time. I'm very early on. You don't have to chip in any money unless you want. And I don't mind going alone. Everything is more cut and dried that way."

"You're pregnant?"

"There's a clinic not too far from where I live. I've passed it a few times on my way to the convenience store. I'll get suctioned, and everything will be back to normal."

"But I don't want you to get an abortion. I think this is great news. Oh God, I'm so fucking happy."

She began to cry. "Stop it, Vic. Please don't be cruel to me. I can't tell you how weak I feel all over. Every cell of my body aches. I know you're angry about the news, but there's no need to be sarcastic. We promised to be kind to one another. I'm trying to make this as easy for you as I can. Maybe that's why I came along, to work up the courage to tell you, instead of writing you a letter."

"I'm not being sarcastic. I really am happy. I didn't think I would be, but I'm overjoyed. Let's find a doctor tomorrow, somewhere around here, and he can at least give us an approximate due date."

Andrea stood regarding him in incredulous silence for a moment. "Well I'm not overjoyed. I'm not overjoyed at all. This couldn't have come at a worse time. Things are complicated to say the least. I have to go back to teaching in a couple of weeks, I can't keep food down even when I try, and my personal life is completely screwed up. My father's going to be furious with me about his MG. And in case you've forgotten, you and I have split."

"But only a few weeks ago. Think of it as a leave of absence. This changes everything."

She shook her head. "Oh, Vic, you're such a creature of the moment. Today you say you want a baby. Tomorrow you'll be wanting to open a miniature golf course down here. This is not how you bring a child into the world. You don't have the least idea of what's involved. I don't either."

"Have you told anybody else about this?"

You're the only one I feel an obligation to tell, because I know you're the father."

"Andrea, I'm really serious about wanting this baby. It's not a whim. I think we can work things out. But if you aren't ready for one, I'll raise it myself. You might change your mind and want one later. Don't you remember giving me that same advice when I called you on the phone out in Arizona?"

"Well, the fetus just happens to be inside my womb. Have you forgotten that?"

"At least think about keeping the baby. Please. We don't have to decide right now."

"I don't know. So I'll think about thinking about it. Only to give you a little more time to realize for yourself what a bad idea it is."

When they got back to the campsite, the four kayakers were passed out.

Beef and Keith had fallen asleep, lying huddled together, her arm flung over his sleeping bag. Vic and Andrea crawled into their respective bags. As he lay against the bed of gravel, Vic wondered if he would ever get a good night's rest again in his life. He heard Andrea's regular sighs already. He alone remained awake, as usual. The campfire had consumed itself almost completely, to the point where a flat red layer of heat oscillated along a thick bed of ashes. It was producing a lot of smoke, which had permeated the area around the site with the bitter stench of charred wood. Vic could taste it in the roof of his mouth. He thought about getting up to douse the fire, so the smoke would dissipate, but the weather had turned cooler still, and he might need to stir the fire back up in the middle of the night and add more wood to keep everybody from catching a chill. So he let it lie.

Wind soughed through the palm trees, making a racket. Behind the dense bank of night clouds, a lowering luminescence rippled at irregular intervals. He would have called it heat lightning, because no roll of thunder followed any of the flashes, not that he could hear. But it was too cold for heat lightning. Maybe this was the severely delayed reaction of the thunderclaps he'd heard in the Rockies. Except that the thunderclaps should come last instead of first. Maybe the whole phenomenal universe was slightly out of kilter. Well, even if it was, what was he going to do about it? He sank down with abandon into the succouring folds of sleep.

Something pinged off his face. A mosquito? No, there were probably no mosquitos here. Too dry for insects of almost any kind. And a mosquito couldn't have landed in this wind, even if there had been one. Besides, whatever it was had left a moist streak on his cheek. Had he caught a catnap? He thought so, because the embers looked dimmer. Had hours passed, or seconds? It pinged again, and pinged again. The sky was purple-yellow as a bruise. Scooting out of his sleeping bag, he stood up in his underwear, defying the elements. A soft hissing descended all around him. "Hey you guys," he said in a stage whisper to no one person in particular. "You'd better get up."

He had no time to elaborate, because at that instant, the heavens poured forth. Rain sloshed down on the slumberers, hammered, washed, practically drove Vic sideways. In a matter of seconds he could see, barely see, puddles forming among the pebbles around his feet. The fire had definitely gone out. Everyone staggered about, half-awake, half-sleepwalking, dragging sleeping bags that weighed a ton and looked like sections of a bloated anaconda they had hacked to death. "I got a monster hang-over," he heard one of the kayakers mutter.

Another one, the climatologist, was more philosophical about the whole business, now that he was already drenched. He meandered over to Vic dripping streamers of water from nose and elbows, and said, "I guess I was wrong about that one inch a year. We're going to turn our kayaks upside down and crawl underneath them. If you guys don't want to sleep in your van, there's a motel in Bahía about eight kilometers south along this road. It's the first one you'll get to. Just bear to your right when you start seeing houses."

Vic thanked the climatologist. His own party was in hysterical motion. Opening the doors of Keith's van, they threw sleeping bags inside without bothering to stuff them back in their sacks. Water got flung everywhere as they pitched their belongings atop one another. Then they all piled in and took off along the service road in search of the motel. The windows steamed up from the inside, and the road had begun to turn to mud, so they couldn't go very fast. Keith kept wiping his sleeve along the inner surface of the windshield. The defroster blew cold air full blast and all the windows were open. The van's wheels spun and fishtailed, throwing spumes of muck to either side. A heavy silence reigned, as if they were all four listening hard for a dislodged stone and a faint click of realignment in the chassis beneath them.

Once the motel came into view, they all went into the lobby together, damp and impatient. The desk clerk, who had a late-night news station turned up loud, seemed amused by their predicament. Everything he said sounded faintly supercilious. Andrea wanted to know whether they had two rooms.

"Two rooms? We have *lots* of rooms. But you mean unoccupied ones, of course. I'd be thrilled to show you the ones that don't have people in them."

"Just give us any two. It doesn't matter."

"Make that three," said Keith.

"Oh, so now it's three? Are you expecting a late arrival?"

"I want to sleep by myself."

"So do I," said the desk clerk. "So do I. But I have to stay up all night every night putting other people to bed." He motioned for them to follow, and led them down the hall. The bulb in the hall was burned out, but he had brought a flashlight. "I've got three right together here." He spot-lighted each door in turn with the flashlight, like a game-show host apprising them of their options. "That way, if you need to communicate with each other in the middle of the night, you can just knock on the wall. The outer walls of the motel are like a fortress, but the inner ones are thin as paper."

The motel clerk opened their doors for them, and loitered around waiting to see who was going to go into what room. Andrea slipped into the farthest one and shut the door behind her. Keith did likewise with the nearest one. Vic and Beef were left standing in the hallway with the flashlight-bearing clerk. "Your turn," he said, smiling.

The walls of the room were made of fake moonrock, like the painted styrofoam boulders in displays at archeological museums. The bed, a double, visibly sagged in the middle and was covered by a spread that had obviously been washed many times, though none too recently. The smell of mildew hung in the air. Faux French doors in one wall led to nowhere. The tiny, antiquated TV was bolted down to a table with what looked like steel rivets for a skyscraper, as if the management expected the place to be trashed by demented rock stars on a budget holiday, and had taken preventive measures. Vic got straight into bed and turned his back to the middle so that he faced out. He closed his eyes and began making regular sighing sounds while Beef got out of her wet clothes, to give the impression that he had fallen quickly into a deep sleep. The way Beef banged into the dresser and grunted while she struggled out of her clothing, he could tell she was still fairly drunk and stoned.

When she got into her side of the bed, the box springs made infernal, stygian creaks. She clicked off the lamp. The bed wasn't particularly narrow, but the indentation in the middle made them roll toward one another so that their backs and shoulders touched. Motes of dust floating about in the dark were palpable. Even though the room had no window, they could hear the rain gushing forth in muffled torrents, flaying the outer wall. There was an expectant, wakeful heaviness on her side of the bed. Please, please, he thought. Please fall asleep. One of her hands searched him out, playing with the nape of his neck and counting the vertebrae of his bare back. Vic squinched up his lids until his eyeballs trembled in their sockets, as if that might make his secular prayer more efficacious.

He turned over to tell her he wasn't in the mood, and they began to kiss. She was naked. Gone was the lurching, tugging, adolescent ferocity of their previous encounter. All that remained was tender sweetness. She hugged him tightly, tightly, but not as if she wanted to crush him. After she let go, she nuzzled her face and hair against his neck, and belly, and cock, and legs, ever so softly. Both of them sat up and he held her face in his hands, gazing at her in the unadulterated darkness and planting kisses on her forehead. When they lay down together, there was a yielding up on her part that he hadn't felt before. A sadness, as if he were going to die the next day, and she knew it, and was giving him one last night of love. Her tenderness frightened Vic. She didn't have any words to say. Instead she moaned, the sounds coming out of her animal and funereal. She moaned like a woman dying for love, or, more precisely, the woman of a man who was going to die for love, through no doing of his own. She moaned as if she wanted the whole world to hear. And all the world probably did hear, or some of it anyway, as it crouched in solitude beyond the paper-thin walls of their rented bedroom.

By morning, the storm had relented. Clouds remained, but orange-white, with only tinges of black. A bluish cast had bled through the sky. The atmosphere felt less crackly. Continuous gusts blew, steady, playful and caressing, almost a sub-tropical tradewind. The downpour had washed months, perhaps years, of lingering dust out of the air, leaving behind the clean scent of freshened plants.

Vic was the first to arise, and he took breakfast in the patio, drinking entirely too many cups of coffee. He was hoping Andrea would come down next, so they would have a chance to talk, and so he could gauge how she was feeling, and whether she had changed her mind. The coffee was making him jumpy. He picked up one of the Mexican newspapers, leafed through to the comic page, and started reading the absurd Spanish-language bubbles above the mouths of Blondie and Dagwood, as the couple worked through another of their perpetual domestic conundrums, the ones that always made Dagwood's hair stand on end and gave him that surprised look. *Dagwood, despiértate! Te llama el Señor Dithers! Está furioso! Ay, Blondie, dónde pusiste mi maletín!*

But somehow or other things always worked out, Mr. Dithers would rant and rave and hop around stamping his oversized feet, yet he continued to dole out the paychecks all the same, year after year, without even having to adjust for inflation, and Dagwood's health didn't seem to deteriorate despite the perennial knockdown-dragouts with various and sundry buck-toothed door-to-door salesmen working on straight commission. Blondie, with her mien of a chirpy and domesticated chorus girl, saw him through, they slept with their backs to each other, she had given up her dissolute life in showbiz long ago, all that shameful past was behind her, and Dagwood, ever circumspect, ever forgiving, wasn't going to bring it up. They always shared one pure kiss before turning over to go to sleep. Vic suspected that they had a decent sex life, missionary style but heartfelt and loving, perhaps on stolen Sunday afternoons, after Dagwood had performed all of his job tasks around the yard, and before he took a nap on the sofa.

Beef sauntered in, and Andrea followed not long after. There was no sign of Keith. The ubiquitous clerk, who'd arisen from his cot behind the front desk and invited himself to sit down at their table, was telling them about various options for entertaining themselves. They could do sport fishing, snorkeling, they could tour the islands in a boat. Something about his descriptions made the activities sound vaguely disreputable. He knew all the appropriate people, and a single phone call by him would deliver these pleasures over to them instantaneously.

When Keith didn't appear, and didn't appear, Beef began to worry. By suffering the hotel clerk's leering sarcasm for a few more minutes, they managed to persuade him to use the passkey to open the door to Keith's room. He wasn't there, and the clerk hadn't seen him go out. When they checked outside, though, Keith's van was gone.

Andrea's expression had shown some faint interest in the idea of going out on a boat. It was only a flicker across her face, but it was enough for Vic. "Look, we don't have any wheels until he gets back. Let's rent a boat and driver for a half day, to go fishing and snorkeling in the Sea of Cortez. It's only forty dollars, dirt cheap. I've got that much left over from the flea market. When we get back, we'll start asking around for Gamma Ray."

The clerk, seconding the motion, said that the motel could pack a picnic lunch for them of fried fish sandwiches, fruit, and boiled eggs for a very reasonable sum. If their companion returned before they did, another boat could take him out to where they were. That was absolutely no problem. Beef seemed distracted. Almost absently, she agreed to go along on the excursion.

The clerk found someone willing to take them out, a local fisherman who worked part-time as a guide for tour groups. Business had been slow lately, it had been dropping off steadily the past few years, and the fisherman seemed happy to accomodate them, especially when he found out that all three of them spoke some Spanish. He shuttled them to the stretch of water where his boat was docked, gaily painted a nautical white and blue. For a few extra dollars, he had all the equipment they needed, snorkels, masks, fins, wet suits. One of the señoritas looked kind of thin, but he could find something to fit her if he rummaged around. That was his business.

If they hadn't brought their own rods and tackle, all he had was heavy rods, more deep-sea type like the ones used on commercial boats, with lead sinkers. They couldn't hope to snag yellowtail or any of the real fighting fish, but they could try for bottom feeders, rock cod, and ling cod. You could at least find some two or three kilo ones this time of year. If they weren't experienced fishermen—ah, and fisher*women* too, of course, he didn't mean to exclude the señoritas—bottom feeders were probably the surest thing anyway, because with the water and sediment all stirred up from last night's freak storm, there was no telling where the fish might be congregating. Around here it rained so infrequently that none of the locals, not even him, could predict for sure what the effects of such a downpour might be on the currents and tides. Everybody was acting jittery and superistitous this morning; none of the fishermen wanted to go out in their boats until things settled down.

Ah, but all the better for them, because they'd have the whole sea to themselves. He knew the best spots, he said as he held up rubber wetsuits to size them, unlocked the shed where the rods were kept, and carefully arranged all the tackle and gear in the boat. If they had bathing suits under their clothes, they could put the wetsuits on later, no sense in getting all dried out and uncomfortable wearing them in the boat. But they'd need them, because the water in the Sea of Cortez got pretty cold. He helped each of them step into the stern, ripped his twin Evinrude engines a few times, and trolled out of the dry-rotted harbor, where the sea had disgorged some of its flotsam among the pilings.

He had to shout above the throb of the motors as he notched them up. The harbor began to recede more quickly. Lucas, that is, himself, would personally guarantee they'd catch more fish today than they'd know what to do with, they didn't have to worry about that. They could fish for a couple of hours, snorkel and swim a couple, go to two or three different spots to see where the fish were biting best, take in the scenery, break the morning up however they wanted.

The water was a deep inky blue, almost black, with only an occasional patch of green. The nearer islands, or islets really, were low and rounded, and from a distance looked like the humps of sedentary whales. When they passed close by one, Vic could see that the islet was probably made from volcanic rock, with so many points and peaks jutting out every which way that only birds could stand comfortably on any part of it. And there were plenty of those—pelicans perched like comical gargoyles, and gulls soaring out for a slow, desultory loop, following in the boat's wake for a moment or two before returning to their austere roosts. Andrea was in unexpected high spirits, standing up in the bow, wind in her eyes, pointing out vistas, taking stabs at identifying flora and fauna, shouting questions at their guide, leaning far over to trail her hand in the water.

Beef seemed subdued, preoccupied, yet trying to enter into the experience in her own quiet way, scanning the horizon for awhile, then migrating over to the other side to do the same to the land. Lucas cut one engine, then the other, and let the boat drift sideways until the currents had settled it. Seagulls chittered in the sudden silence as waves knocked the craft gently to and fro. Lucas wrapped a length of fishing twine around his hand, dangled it in the water, and when he got a nibble, pulled a small fish in with a single yank. Skinning and fileting it in a few quick strokes with a hunting knife, he cut the meat into shreds and threw it in a pail, to use for bait. "Some people buy commercial bait, but I say fish eat fish. Nothing they like better." He baited their hooks for them and handed around the stiff, heavy, cumbersome rods.

"Ever fish before?" All of them shook their heads. Vic had been once,

on a deep sea excursion, but he'd gotten sick right at the beginning and
hadn't gotten to do any fishing. "Okay, since we're just looking for cod,
take your line straight to the bottom. Don't make it dance around in the
water. Push in the button on the side there, let the line pay out, keeping
your thumb on it so it doesn't get tangled up. It will go a long, long way
down, and you'll feel a thump when the sinker hits. Then reel it in a few
notches to get the sinker off the sea floor. The fish will do the rest. When
you feel you've got a bite, reel in slow and steady, so it doesn't struggle off
the hook. Soon as you see the head and gills appear, stop reeling, hoist the
pole up easy, take hold of the fish with your free hand, and give it a big wet
kiss on the mouth. Nah, I'm just teasing there ladies, about that last thing."

The first few casts, Vic found himself too eager, sensing phantom bites
that would cause him to crank for what seemed a full five minutes, only to
watch the shreds of bait come shooting out of the water on the end of his
barbed hooks. His arms were already tired out before he got his first real
nibble. Once he settled into the rhythm and caught one or two, though, he
came up with a catch almost every time after that, sometimes two or three
fish at once. It was an eerie sensation to feel the fish go through its
underwater contortions, thrashing invisibly for several minutes, and have it
appear out of the deep all at once, only when it was already practically in the
boat. It didn't take Vic long to realize that this wasn't sport fishing at all; it
was just easy pickings. Lucas had judged his customers well. He probably
knew by now that there were fewer human varieties than there were ones of
fish, six or seven at most, and had figured them—correctly, Vic thought—
for the type who'd be happy to catch a lot of fish right off in a hurry and get
the task over with, so they could go out and play in the water.

By wrapping his shirt around his hand, he covered the small spot he'd
burned on the metal can, which had already started to heal, so that he
hardly even noticed it. The dull ache there only made him realize how
good the rest of him felt. The midmorning sun had come out strongly for
short periods, warming his bones. He remained only vaguely and drowsily
aware of the figure of Lucas removing each fish from their hooks as it came
up to the surface, so his tourists could cast their lines right back in; of the
fish piling up behind him in the boat; of the lazy conversation between
Lucas and Beef about the geological history of the area, something or other
about volcanic deposits, fiery movements of earth being torn asunder, and

how, on account of the mineral layers, you could tell that all the islands used to be a part of the peninsula before their violent dislocation.

Once in a while Vic and Andrea would turn to smile at one another, without premeditation, like two children who share a private joke they know is silly by adult standards, but that makes them want to burst out laughing anyway. Whatever she had thought last night, whatever she had heard as she lay separate in her motel room, whatever wildly shifting set of scenarios had played across her mind, all that anguish was behind her now, or maybe not all, but the worst part of it anyway. She didn't appear to be holding anything against him, lapses recent or distant. Another state of mind seemed to be asserting itself slowly, holding gradual sway, subsuming all else, drawing her into a wider and more forgiving stream of possibilities. Once, she reached over discreetly, after depositing a fish behind her, and patted his leg.

He was tying on a new lead sinker to replace the one he'd lost by getting it entangled in something, when he saw the blur of animal presence fly out of the water at the end of Andrea's hook. The tiny, grappling fish was as orange-red and angry looking as an infected boil. It had an armor of spikes radiating out from its body, and as Andrea lurched backward to avoid getting hit, her line snapped taut and sent the spiky fish whipping about Vic's head like a mace. It landed in the boat and continued to writhe, gouging the cod lying there.

"Don't anybody touch it," said Lucas. "Let me take it off the hook."

"What is it?"

"A scorpion fish. You don't want to get one of those spines lodged in you. That little mother's full of poison. Worse than stepping on a coral reef. Make your foot blow up like an innertube, and just as black." He pried open the scorpion fish's mouth to work out the lodged hook, holding the fish as carefully as if he were defusing a bomb. "No sense keeping this one. It's not worth prying off all that skin. The meat will just make you sick to your stomach." He threw the scorpion fish back in the water. Taking off his billed cap and wiping his face with it, he smiled at them, the casual smile of somebody who has just saved the world from thermonuclear destruction, and can afford to smile that way. "Well, caramba. I was going to take you all around to two or three more places, so you could get your quota of fish. But you're too good. " He held his arms out to his sides deferentially, giving the trio their just due. "Before we pull up any more scorpion fish, we better scoot on over to one of the bigger, more sheltered islands so you can take a swim. If we catch any more cod, we have to throw them back anyway. You're over the limit."

They reeled in their lines, he put the boat on full throttle, and they traversed a stretch of open sea, the front of their craft reared high in the water. As the island came into sight, its stark eastern shore rose in sheer cliffs to a volcanic mesa. Serpentine valleys ran down through it into coves that looked from the distance like they might have sand beaches. "We'll go on around to the southern shore. All the coves are beautiful, but there's a nice, well-protected one I especially like as you round the tip to the southern side."

The island looked to have been formed out of petrified lava flows. Strata were visible in the cliff walls, yellow, coral, rust, white, volcanic black, running in strictly separated bands. The minerals looked soft as sandstone, the faces were eroded into a kind of lacework, and Vic couldn't help thinking how the facets of the island reminded him of the buttes carved out by the wind in Arizona. A few of the black bands zigzagged in a crazy tilt down the rock face, disappearing below the water line. "Yeah, there must have been one heck of a big blast a long time ago, that raised these islands straight out of the sea," said Lucas. "Hard to imagine."

"Does anybody live on them?"

"No, you couldn't really. Too harsh, even by Baja standards. But there did used to be pearl divers who lived out here, a couple or three centuries back, not too long after old Cortez himself came out this way. They brought up black pearls, mostly, before the combination of natives and settlers completely fished that variety of oyster straight out of existence. The padres, they didn't mind the *indios* making a living that way, long as they gave the Virgin a hefty cut of what they hauled up each day as an offering. Protection racket, you know. But one of these young *machos* didn't want to cooperate, said the *quinta* wasn't his lookout, and one day when he dove down to search for pearls he didn't come back up. His *compadres* went after him to see what was keeping him, and found the young *macho* clamped by one leg in the jaws of a giant clam. These other divers ran quick as they could to make a token offering to the Virgin of that last pearl he grabbed, to try to save his soul from damnation. That's what people say, anyway. A few schemers have tried to revive the pearl diving industry a few times, off and on, because the economy's so dead down here. You come across heaps of mother-of-pearl shells on the islands once in a while, or rusted-out cages in the water, but the pearl thing never really took off again. So we fish and haul you gringos around instead. It's a living."

"Is that true, the story about the pearl diver?"

Lucas popped open a can of Seven Up, chugalugged it, and tossed it overboard. "Look, I don't have nothing against the Virgin. She's a nice lady and all, and she never did anything bad to me. But if the señoritas will excuse the expression, I think it's a lot of b.s. Good to have a few stories like that in your repertoire, though. Some of the fishing parties really get off on that exotic stuff, especially if it's an overnight trip, and they've been passing around the tequila after dark. Hey, but you guys better watch out. After the wild storm last night, and with all the muck stirred up, some of those giant clams might be in a bad mood. That's probably the real reason why nobody's out on the water today." He cackled. "Okay, we're pulling into the cove now. I'm going to park on the sandbar off to the right, because I don't want the rocks busting up my boat. You all can wade in to shore from there, and I'll throw you your wetsuits and gear so you can dress."

As Andrea stood on shore, her flesh not quite filling her Speedo, trying to work the dry rubber wetsuit over her legs, she began to shiver visibly. After washing his hands in the surf, Lucas opened the enchiladas he had stashed in his waterproof box, and started eating them. But then he re-wrapped the enchiladas in brown paper, grabbed a mesh bag from under his seat, and waded onto the beach without rolling up his pants. "You look a little cold there already, señorita."

"Are you sure you're up to this?" Vic asked her.

"I'd be fine," she answered, her teeth chattering, "if I could shake this chill." Her hair wet and straggly, she looked forlorn. "I don't want to be left behind," she said. "I've been looking forward to this all morning."

"Here, try this on. It's called a cheater vest. Slip it underneath your wetsuit, and it gives your upper body an extra layer of warmth. I use one myself sometimes." Lucas helped her slip into it, as solicitous as a father pinning a corsage on his daughter's breast. "Sit over there on the sunny part of the beach and have a bite of something to eat first. You'll feel better soon. I'm kind of chilly myself. You want part of my enchilada?"

She sat in the sand in her wetsuit, soaking up sun and devouring boiled eggs, fish sandwiches, enchiladas, and several bananas. She ate all of her lunch, part of Lucas's, and most of Vic's. Vic tried to offer Lucas some of his remaining lunch, but Lucas waved it off, patting his stomach. "I'm getting too much of a tire anyway. My wife cooks too good. Or here," he said, squatting down and attaching his sheathed hunting knife with snaps right above one of Vic's nylon boots. "I'm going to loan you this so you can catch me my lunch. I'm in the mood for some steamed clams." He winked. "I prefer the real big ones."

By the time Andrea finished eating, she was practically panting. She looked more content. Vic could also tell that the extreme tightness of the wetsuit on her limbs and torso, the way she filled it, was satisfying to her. She took an almost ecstatic pleasure in clothing that adhered to her body like a second skin. Beef hadn't yet changed into her suit, and at last she came up to him, saying, "I don't think I'll go snorkeling with you two."

"Not go with us? Why not?"

She avoided his eyes, tossing her hair over her left shoulder and gazing back in the general direction they'd come from. "I don't even know why I'm telling you this. Guess I'm acting just like you. Right before the storm, when you and Andrea went off down the beach, I did it with one of those kayakers. Not even made love—just did it. Maybe because I was pissed at you, maybe because I was stoned."

"You don't have to confess anything to me, Beef. You've been nothing but generous to me."

"I don't know about that. I got what I wanted, I guess. As well as some things I didn't especially want. That's the way it usually works out with me. Anyway, Lucas was telling me that on some of the smaller islands we passed on our way here, there are shelves made up completely of seashells. I was remembering that I'd promised my next door neighbor Francisco that I'd bring him back some shells for his rock garden. He's very meticulous about his landscaping, and I'd like to find him some big unbroken ones."

"Sure, go ahead. I think it's a great idea. If you don't make it back here before we're finished swimming, I guess I'll see you on the return trip. Unless you want us to go over there with you to snorkel?"

"No, that's okay. This looks like a nice spot. It just doesn't have what I'm looking for. We'll all ride back together, in any case."

Vic knew she was going to return to shore to look for Keith, but he said nothing to let on that he did. Beef, for her part, knew why he wanted to stay here, but she said nothing more about that either. He walked down the beach to where Lucas had just finished taking a leak behind some rocks. Vic handed him all of the money in his billfold. "I want to go ahead and pay you. Thank you for everything," he said. "I hope this is a good enough tip. You've been wonderful to us. This is the happiest day of my life." There were tears in his eyes as he spoke. He felt like a newly married man giving money to a pimp.

Lucas pocketed the money without counting it. "On the contrary, thank you, señor," he said. He was thoroughly professional, from the bill of his baseball cap down to the tips of his huaraches. "The other señorita told me she wants to go foraging for seashells. I know all the best places. I can come pick you up around one o'clock." Lucas looked at his watch, a skin-diver model with a thick crystal and lots of dials. "That's two hours from now. Is that enough time for what you need to do?"

"Yes. Two hours is an eternity."

"All right," he said, walking back down the beach. "The two of you need to be very careful," he half-yelled, in the tone of voice a lifeguard uses to give instructions to a pool full of noisy children. "The water's pretty calm right now, but it can be deceptive. It turns rough in a big hurry when even a few clouds blow up. Especially the day after a storm, you can see the waves are still kind of choppy. You both know how to swim okay?"

"We're both good swimmers," said Vic. "Especially her. Back in college, they used to call her Madame Butterfly."

"That so? Well, I never heard of that person, but I guess she must be a good swimmer too. I'd stay close around the beach if I was you, but if you're wanting to see the more colorful fish, you'll have to go out a little ways. If you do swim toward those groups of rocks or islets, stay to the landward side, where it's more protected. And just remember, some of those rock formations are sharp as razors, and the currents around them can be pretty wicked. If you're near one, and you feel the current drawing you toward it, don't try to fight. That's your natural instinct, but all you'll do is wear yourself out and get cut to ribbons. If you just make your body go relaxed, and don't panic, nine times out of ten the current will carry you around the rocks and into calmer water. You got that?"

"Yes," said Vic. "What about the tenth time?"

"The tenth time?" He shrugged. "You just kiss your behind goodbye. You got that, señorita?"

"Yes."

"Okay then, tall señorita, let's you and me go on a treasure hunt." They clambered from the sandbar into the boat and he started up the engines. The echoing walls of the cove amplified the roar. "Oh yeah," he yelled over the reverberating noise, waving merrily as the boat pulled away. "One more thing. Watch out for those giant clams!"

Vic and Andrea put on their masks and fins and walked stiff-legged together down into the sea. The land fell away, the shallows dropped off quickly, and soon they were forced to become horizontal if they wanted to make any forward progress. The hollow rubber tubing in their mouths allowed them to remain under the surface and yet still breathe. Once in a while, a stray wave would funnel salt water into his snorkel, stinging the back of his throat, and he'd have to blow it clear to keep from choking. The drops left inside would make a phlegmy rattle for a few breaths until they, too, disappeared. But for the most part, the medium felt congenial, effortless, hospitable. The climatologist had been right. The water seemed especially saline and buoyant. It kept trying to push them up to the surface, where tubular, almost invisible sea creatures streaked along, a hair below the waterline. He and she had to stroke their arms upward to keep their bodies underwater.

The sea bottom spread out before them, mossy green and dappled with daylight like the floor of a cedar forest. The water was so murky and oxygenated with the movements of their limbs that it was hard to see very far ahead. The spires of rock reefs appeared beneath them, almost close enough to scrape their bellies, but when Vic reached out to touch one he found they were much further away than they appeared. Turning his mask toward Andrea, he signalled that they should do a short dive to see what lay further down. She assented, her eyes smiling and eager, the hard rubber mouthpiece sealed beneath her lips. Vic let his legs float upward until he was almost vertical, and then, holding his breath, he began to beat the water above him with his fins, and made wide flailing arcs with his arms to propel him downward out of the cocoon of bubbles he'd created. She did the same, only a second or two behind him.

The murkiness gave way to almost total clarity as they neared the bottom. They closed in on the rock reef nearest them, circling the shallow hollow it made, a niche not deep, but enough so to make a shelter for the silvery minnows and translucent tetras that swayed within it, a peculiar combination of motion and stillness. Shelves of gunmetal mineral lay littered here and there along the bottom like quarrystone rubble, half-obscured by motes and threads of plankton eddying about. There was no profusion of tropical color, no coral reefs or schools of rainbow parrotfish as gaudy in color as their namesakes. A lone angelfish striped yellow, black, and blue, wandered in and out of breaks in the reef, and clumps of seaweed waved, dark as spinach leaves, in pale yellow light. Vic and Andrea let their bodies rise, let the salinity buoy them up again, and just as they began to reach the surface together, blew spumes of water to clear their breathing tubes.

"Synchronicity," she said, letting the mouthpiece fall from her mouth and laughing. "It's beautiful down there. Let's go a little further out along the cove and try again." Vic nodded. The sun broke forth, illuminating oceanic expanses for an instant, making them glitter, then withdrew again just as easily, leaving behind a slate gray color. She led the way, fins flashing. Vic watched her move off before he followed. Her calves and haunches pumped along in perfect rhythm. She had the best form he'd ever seen on anyone. There was no unnecessary torsion, no skewing, no wasted motion. She displaced the greatest amount of water with the least amount of effort, virtually parting the waters. When he submerged himself again, and straightened out his length below the surface, he spied the twin white trailers left by her fins. Once he had caught up with her, or rather, once she had let him, she pointed downward, and they inverted their bodies again, making their watery handstands last all the way down. The sea floor there was made of coarse tan sand, speckled with black and white flecks. Noticing faint protruberances in the ground, Vic cleared off topsand with his fingers and discovered clams embedded there. Reaching down to his calf, he drew the knife out of its sheath and pried loose one, two, three of them. He handed one to Andrea, who turned it over in her fingers to inspect it, gazing through the lens of her mask with a jeweler's concentration. Placing the clam in her other hand, she held it aloft like a pearl, a really fine one she was showing off, then clutched it in her palm and shot to the top. Drifting up and breaking the surface, he found her there, looking amused, mask pushed back, eyes twinkling as she dog-paddled to stay afloat.

"It's mine now," she said. "It's hidden somewhere on my person, but you'll never find it unless you look very hard for it. Once you make an offering to the Virgin, you can't go back on it."

He pushed back his own mask, letting the snorkel dangle in its holder. "Oh, yes I can. I stuck the other two in my boot to prove to Lucas that I really can hunt clams. But the one you have, the choice one, is merely on loan. It's the most priceless gem in our collection. The rare black pearl, of which there is only one in the world."

She stretched out her neck and gave him a salty kiss. The way the waves were knocking him about, he had to perform a strenuous frog-kick in order to stay aloft. Their teeth clacked. She shook her head. "Pearls before swine." Pulling her mask back on, she said, "Let's swim out to one of the islets."

"Are you sure you're feeling strong enough for such a long swim? You ate a lot of lunch and you might get stomach cramps. Maybe we should just play along the cove."

"Am I strong enough? The way you splash around like a one-legged duck, you're the one who's going to peter out before we get there. I feel great. This cold water is exhilarating. Tonight I'm going to eat a steak as thick as your arm. Come on, I'll race you."

She lowered her head and was off in a silent streak, the water folding in behind her as she went. In a choppy swath of inefficient motion, he tried to catch her. She knew he never would, but she let him struggle for a while, made him go through the exertions before she slacked off at last and let him fall in next to her. Now they swam easily together, in deeper, colder water. All the reefs had slanted too far down to be seen. An occasional underwater dune undulated up to within sight, but after a time even those were gone. Fish, larger and more exotic ones, appeared out of the void at intervals and disappeared again. They manifested themselves to his mind as iridescent streaks or floating masses of shining symmetrical scales, but for all their spectacular markings, he couldn't really tell one from the other. She, not he, had always been the one with the gift for naming. And when the time came, she, not he, would choose the name. Having been given a creature's bare existence, he didn't really care what it was called. It floated there in its amniotic sphere, surrounded by fluid and still more fluid, membranous, permeable, undifferentiated. Or, he supposed, it was differentiated, but it kept its own counsel, waiting patiently, secure and unhurried in the simple fact of its being. That was the best way.

He swam out of time, feeling the fins flex at the tips of his legs, with nothing below him or above, and only the black silhouette of Andrea moving beside him in perfect synch, a shadow in his peripheral vision. The burble of their mutual breath made a ripple in the silence, but otherwise, it remained absolute, and he was glad. There were a lot of complications still to be worked through, but they didn't seem especially daunting, or even difficult. All he knew, all that concerned him, was that she and he were together. He had won her back, despite himself, almost by accident. He loved that word now. Fate had thrown an accident in their mutual way, and they would see to the rest. The whole universe had been an accident, if you wanted to look at it in that light, a chancy, freakish, random combination of elements that sorted itself out into elegant taxonomies only after the fact. The question of his relationship with Beth, he had to call her Beth at this moment, existed in Vic's mind only as a parting of the ways, hazy and numbing as the greenish water he swam through. It would simply happen, with a sort of simultaneous sigh of regret, and then they wouldn't see one another after that, perhaps ever again.

More rock reefs were becoming visible, little archipelagoes at an unfathomable distance. They came progressively closer, and soon she and he were surrounded by sedimentary shelves, having to split to either side at times to skirt their uppermost branches. The current had turned tidal and strong, washing their bodies about, and they had to swim hard to keep from being brought up against reefs encrusted with barnacles and mollusks. Lifting their heads above the waterline, they saw the islet before them, foaming with surf. They backpaddled until they were relatively free of the current drawing them toward it. It looked almost like an atoll, curving into itself, with what appeared to be a little strip of beach at one end. Banks of protoplasmic, charcoal cloud above them fused together and disengaged, throwing ephemeral, mile-long shadows like nets across the patch of sea where they swam, and dredging them back empty. A frigid freshet of air swept across the water's surface, and Vic shivered.

"Whew. I just realized I'm freezing my ass off. My bones hurt, and even the fillings in my teeth ache. You can probably see my goosebumps through my wetsuit."

She shivered too, but it looked to be a delicious shiver. Her skin was flushed, taut without seeming strained or glassy, and she had a big smile on her face. "Colder than a witch's tit," she said. "Care to feel one? Are you feeling horny? Got that clammy little newt down there warmed up yet?"

He laughed. "Well, I'll make you a deal. If you can find it, we'll do it. But all I can say is, good luck."

"Hmm. In that case, let's swim around the islet."

"Okay. If you want to. My arms are tired, though. Aren't you starting to feel the swim?"

"I'm just getting my second wind. But I'll handicap you. I'll do a modified butterfly stroke, snorkel gear and all."

"No, let's not race. The water's too rough here. Let's just skirt the islet, making sure we stay to the landward side and clear of any narrows."

"Come on. Stop acting so much like an expectant father." They meandered among the miniature archipelagoes surrounding the islet, trying to stay down as deep as they could, where the water remained smoother and less erratic. Andrea kept wending through the narrowest passes with her slender frame and turning back to dare him through with a sweep of her arm. More often than not he had to push himself off the rock surfaces, and though he couldn't actually see any blood, he felt a few tiny slits thin as paper cuts on his fingers. It was silly, he knew, but he couldn't help wondering whether carnivorous sea creatures could detect the scent of his blood. They scouted around for a while longer, coming up time and again for air, and to check their bearings against both the islet and the bigger island in the near distance, the one they'd come from, to make sure they were staying to the landward side. Then, plunging down again, they came across one of the rusted-out cages Lucas had spoken of, wedged in the mouth of another hollow. The bars of the cage were reddish-green, thick and uneven with encrustations.

When she laid her hand on the oyster cage, a lamprey shot out and swam away into the bluer-hued water beyond, giving them both a fright, but then she signaled to him to help her try to dislodge the cage and take it to the top. He couldn't imagine what she expected to do with it, but she was that way, performing small rituals like this just for the exercise. After going

up for one more breath of air, they dove down and took hold of the edges of
the cage. Threshing the water with their bodies, both hands on the bars,
they tried to yank one corner of it out, then another, but without success.
The water was too thick with salinity, and however great their lung
capacity, they simply couldn't stay under sufficiently long.

She let go, motioning to him that she, too, had had enough. Fluttering
upward to where her snorkel broke the surface, she paddled away from the
reefs toward the open blue water where the lamprey had gone. He followed, a foot or two behind her. The sea, calm and boundless again, spread
out into infinity. He assumed she was ready to head back, and she apparently either had a very keen sense of direction, or was totally disoriented.
He knew he was lost. He wanted to lift his head up to take his bearings
again, but the water was so cloudy, he didn't wish to risk losing sight of her,
even for an instant.

Then she was gone. She didn't vanish, exactly, she simply wasn't there
anymore. He tried not to panic. She would be revealed any second. The
murkiness kept clearing off in places, showing him different shades of aqua-
marine illuminated from the top with daylight, but none of them contained
her. When he lifted his head to try to spot the tip of her snorkel projecting
from the water, he could see plenty of surface waves continuous with the
slate sky, but neither her snorkel, nor the islet, nor the island were
anywhere in sight. He put his head back down. The current had picked up.
He couldn't tell where it was coming from or going to, but wherever the
destination was, it was getting him there faster than before. The water
began to foam, agitating him, tossing him around at will. He sensed that he
was being drawn toward shoals. Even as his terror rose, it almost comforted
him to think that he was going to crash into something solid, something
that would stop his acceleration.

Then the first stone glanced off his face, taking bits of flesh and skin
with it. He cringed and cowered, trying not to fight the current, remembering that Lucas had told him it would carry him around the islet to the
other side. He bobbed and spun, hurtling and backwashing in a lather of
surf and tidal motion. Only twice more did he feel the smash of bruising
hard rock. He was afraid, and yet it seemed a kind of miracle that he still
hadn't died. His mind remained clear, and he knew that he must be
eddying among hundreds of jagged facets of reef, but he seemed to exist in

a turbulent void, a blank chaos. His body collided with something, something more solid than water, less solid than rock, and he knew at once that it was Andrea. Did she also know it was him? He reached out toward her, and in that instant the reefs began to perform their lacerations in earnest. They flayed his limbs and torso, slicing through rubber and skin and he cried out, grappling with Andrea's shrouded form to try to lay hold of her for ballast. His left leg was colossal. A scorpion fish had broken spines off in the flesh of it, and now the leg swelled with poisonous elephantiasis. Or one of the clams inside his boot had grown to gigantic size, and had his foreleg pinned in its maw. It was trying to drag him down. He would be swallowed, and the dark secretions would begin.

He might have screamed, but his throat was in spasms. He groped for the knife strapped to his calf and managed to yank it from its sheath. But all at once there was a sigh, a cosmic loosening, a sort of fatigued letting go. He had been released. He was standing on a sandbar, in water no higher than his waist. Perhaps he'd been in only a few feet of it all along. He watched Andrea's hair and face appear, then her upper torso as she emerged from the sea and staggered toward him. She was battered, bleeding through her cuts like him, and although she didn't speak, she plainly recognized him. There was a look of intensity, of frenzy in her eyes.

And then she seized hold of him to save herself. One arm looped about his neck, and the other grabbed his face. She was dragging him downward, back into the water. She was drowning, or thought she was, it came to the same thing. He wanted to tell her they were okay, they were on safe ground. But now they were both drowning. Her extremities scrabbled over him, lashing like tentacles, merciless, hard, unforgiving. He tried to throw her off, but she was too strong, her adrenaline was flowing, she had superhuman strength. The strength wouldn't last long, just long enough for her to kill him, then she too would go completely limp and the sea would claim her. He realized he still had the hunting knife clutched in his hand. He tried to free his pinned wrist and forearm, so he could get a proper grip, but she was holding onto him for dear life. Her skull cracked against his, he dropped the knife, and somehow he managed to get behind her. They collapsed in a tight embrace and the surf rolled them over and over, the coarse, abrasive particles of sand skinning him through the rips in his wetsuit. When he felt land stick solidly beneath him again, he began to pull her up onto the islet. Half-sitting, half-squatting, still wearing one of his fins, he wrenched her out of the tide with lurching, awkward, fitful, awful, crablike motions.

They lay on the strip of beach, heaving and apart. She had lost both of her fins, and her mask was gone. His lay beside him. Lucas's hunting knife was somewhere out in the surf. Andrea appeared to be conscious, and not that badly off altogether, but he didn't have the strength to get up and check to be sure. If a tongue of surf were to lick up to where she lay and draw her back down into the waves, he would have to let her go. If it did the same to him, he wouldn't have minded that much, or at least he wouldn't have protested very loudly. He wanted to muster up the energy to yell out for the waves to pour over his head. He wanted to shout that they were obliged to, to punish him.

But despite sucking in and out of tidal pools, the whitecaps before them didn't look actively ill-disposed. He was anthropomorphizing, committing the pathetic fallacy, trying to whip up the forces of nature when he barely had breath to spare for himself. If he added a little roseate gloaming, he thought bitterly, the vista would be positvely Homeric. His face throbbed. The gash on his cheek felt as ugly and pointless as a dueling scar. There could well be several; he really couldn't tell. Then again, the reef seemed to have spread the wounds around his body with democratic regularity. They weren't going to kill him, but they would hurt like hell in a couple of hours. The leg that had gotten pinned burned already, huge and hot.

Gulls hopped about in his vicinity, looking bored and dissatisfied in a pea-brained sort of way. Andrea opened her eyes and gave him a weak smile. She looked pretty banged up too. Not mortally so either, but at least as bad as him and perhaps a little worse. "I guess you can't always ream it out," she said.

"How do you feel?"

"Oh, you know. Not bad, all things considered. I feel sheepish, mostly. You know how macho I get sometimes." She laid a hand on her pubic bone and cupped her crotch. "Ow, shit. There it goes again."

"What?" He struggled to his knees.

"When we first got drawn into that hard stream, I was trying to keep my wits about me. But I must have gotten so scared I messed my pants. Now it just happened again. I hope that's the last of it."

"It's involuntary," he said, trying to sound offhand, clinical, as unconcerned as possible. "You can't help it." He crawled over the sand to where she lay. "Let me see." Even against the dark black of the wetsuit, he could detect the stain between her legs when she removed her hand.

"It kind of hurts," she said, her voice all at once fearful and tentative. "It almost feels like cramps."

He lay his head face down in her lap. The smell of her was pungent, hormonal. Vic began to cry, and she stroked his hair. "Fucking Christ," he said. "Fucking, fucking Christ." He had an image of the placenta issuing forth from her into the seawater, diaphanous and elongated like a jellyfish, streamers of blood trailing behind as it drifted away. They lay side by side for a long time, facing upward, as if they had meant to witness an eclipse, and had come out on purpose to a place where they knew the view would be clear and unobstructed. His wetsuit steadily dried and tightened about him. The breezes blew more sharply, but without any real fury, just enough to ensure discomfort. Eventually, they heard a sound and sat up. Lucas's blue and white boat came roaring around from the eastern side of the island. He cut the motors and glided across the cove to the sandbar where he'd parked before.

He was alone. He got out, waded ashore, and scouted the beach, but not for very long. Climbing back into the boat, Lucas backed out of the inlet, swung about, and headed straight for their islet. It was as if he had known and expected from the beginning that they would turn disobedient as soon as they were out of his sight.

Lucas brought a brief but urgent message from Beef telling Vic that his client, Keith Jackson, was being held at the police post in Bahía, that Keith needed the counsel of his attorney at once, and asking him to please make himself as presentable as he could as soon as he could. She didn't know on what charge he was being held exactly, but she would fill him in on the details she did know when he arrived.

Lucas drove Vic and Andrea to the clinic of Bahía, a single ward of half a dozen beds, no larger than the sick bay of a school nurse. Bowls and pitchers sat on washstands beside the beds, and boxes of medications were stored in cabinets that looked like vending machines. A single elderly man with liver spots on his pate lay under covers, eating an orange and reading a magazine. He didn't appear to be in any discomfort. The place was extraordinarily clean, and the energetic nurse on duty seemed almost grateful for an occasion by which she could prove the level of her skill and competence.

The nurse's self-assured but almost cursory manner seemed to put Andrea at ease. She acted relieved to be commended into the nurse's hands, and freed from Vic's messy, tender, ineffectual solicitude. He was as depressed and depleted as her, and it was all he had to offer. The nurse said the doctor would return within the hour. The instruments she used—the thermometer, the blood pressure cup, the stethoscope—looked anachronistic. They were the kind of oversized, antiquarian objects that might have been found on the wall in Keith's house, or spread over his tables at the flea market. Watching her coolly and methodically assess Andrea's condition and take her vital signs with the rudimentary instruments at her disposal made Vic realize that he didn't know the first thing about caring for a sick human being. Whatever knowledge he had acquired in his single year of medical school had long since atrophied, at least with respect to any practical use he might put it to. He couldn't have performed the simple tasks he was watching to save his life, let alone anyone else's.

When the nurse had finished with Andrea, and settled her in bed, she also gave Vic the once over, treated his wounds and abrasions with mercurochrome, put a butterfly bandage on his cheek, and pronounced him sound, though he was welcome to wait until the doctor arrived for a complete diagnosis. "You don't need to hang around, however," she told him rather pointedly. "The young lady seems none for the worse. She's lost a lot of blood, that's true. But she's stable, and we can give her a transfusion right here on the spot if it comes to that. The best thing is to leave her alone for a while and let her get some rest."

"She's right. I feel fine. Go ahead to the police post with Lucas. All I want right now is to eat some lunch and try to sleep a little if I can." She wasn't acting very upset by the events of the day, which probably meant she would be parsing them out for the rest of her life. He felt hurt by her renewed rebuffs. If she had asked him, he would have stayed with her a little longer at least. Keith's troublesome situation, whatever it was, still seemed remote, abstract, less real than what they had just been through together. It had waited this long, it could wait another hour or so until the doctor had a chance to examine her properly and pronounce her in definite good health. But she didn't ask him to stay.

She offered her cheek. He kissed her goodbye, promised he would return as soon as he could, and Lucas drove him to the hotel. He kept apologizing along the way for having lost the snorkel gear and the knife, and for putting Lucas through so much. Lucas told him not to worry about it, that they would settle accounts afterward. He seemed genuinely unconcerned. His detachment from the whole affair was admirable. He assumed that he would either get his due or he wouldn't, that they would reward him handsomely for his trouble, or give him a mere token pittance, or stiff him altogether, and he wasn't going to agonize over which it might turn out to be. He was generous, genuinely generous, not without ulterior motives, but he also didn't seem to bear rancor when things didn't pay off in the way he had calculated. So far, he was operating at a loss on this particular venture. At the same time, he apparently wasn't going to involve himself any more than necessary in the desperate matters in question. He didn't act the least bit curious about knowing what they consisted of, and couldn't give Vic any information about Keith's situation beyond what had been contained in the note from Beef. The gringos on holiday could run amok, wield knives in an improper manner, even live polygamously if they wanted, but that wasn't his lookout. He was a fishing guide, and could serve as an impromptu taxi driver when pressed.

Back at the motel, the urgency referred to in Beef's note began to overtake Vic. He jammed the broken zipper on his suitcase and had to rip it open by main force, which he didn't have much left of. He had a hard time getting the wetsuit to go down over his stiff left leg. He changed into his suit, the one he'd originally draped over a hanger a million years ago; the one he'd meant to wear to the first day of his job in Manhattan. The suit was more wrinkled than ever before. He should have had it dry cleaned while he still had the chance. It was the only piece of halfway presentable clothing he owned, the only chance he had of passing himself off as an attorney. The motel's sole iron had tarry black streaks all along the surface, as if it had been used to seal rubber patches to inflatable lifeboats. So he simply put the suit on the way it was, and had Lucas drive him to the police post.

As he approached the entrance of the tiny building, he recognized the station wagon, more dented and more off-white than ever, but definitely his. The expired license plate on the back confirmed it. Now it was the last thing he wanted to see. He hoped that his and Andrea's implication in this car would not come to light in the course of the interview.

"This is Keith Jackson's attorney," said Beef. "The one I've been telling you about."

The captain looked skeptical. "Quite a shaving cut you've got there."

"I took the morning off to recreate in the ocean. I didn't expect the water to be so rough."

"You should have stayed out on the Sea of Cortez. Things are a lot rougher around here. Today, anyway." The captain spoke these words with a soft, urbane intonation. His uniform was starched and creased, and not a speck of dirt could be found on his cap. Perhaps because he commanded a police post, an outpost at that, rather than a real station, he seemed to strive all the more to ensure that his surroundings stayed civilized. The three desks behind him, and their respective manual typewriters, had been set in perfect alignment. Reams of blank paper were at the ready for processing depositions. A jug of mineral water sat inverted in its stand in one corner, with a stack of matching metal cups next to it. There were only a few notices tacked onto the cork bulletin board, all with secretarial precision.

"You wouldn't happen to have some sort of identification with you?" the captain asked, giving him the once over.

"Like my passport, you mean?" He held it out tentatively, trying his best not to yank it back. To his relief, the captain waved the passport away.

"No, what I had in mind was more of a lawyerly identification. A little plastic card, perhaps, wallet-sized, issued by the accrediting agency of your country? The U.S. seems to be very big on that sort of thing. Not that I'm trying to present the two of you with undue obstacles. I'm simply trying to enforce the law as it's written. This woman claims to be here on behalf of a correctional facility in Utah. As soon as she crossed the threshold, she produced a fistful of documents she wanted me to look at, so that I would give her an interview with the man we have in detention in the next room. But I told her I didn't want to inspect those papers or any others until there was proper legal representation present. In spite of the landscape, this isn't the Wild West. The matter before us is a grave one—murder."

Beef blanched. "Murder?" said Vic.

"Yes. Are you familiar with this client, or is this going to be your first meeting?"

Vic could see that the captain was feeling them out, trying to get a sense of what the relationship among them was without asking directly. "I am," said Vic. He tried to speak with the forceful equanimity the captain seemed to expect of him. "But I was down here on slightly different business, and have just been apprised of this circumstance."

"Exactly what business is that?"

"I'm not sure that's germane to the matter at hand. I'm not the one who's been detained. Or am I under suspicion of having done something wrong? I haven't had a chance to interview my client yet. I hope it's not too much to ask that he give me his side of the story in private before I'm expected to defend him. Or are you going to send me to Mexico City to get a writ of habeas corpus, or whatever you call it down here?"

"Ah, yes. I recognize instantly that subtle combination of deference and sarcastic impatience that attorneys always use when dealing with the servants of public order. If I didn't know better, I'd swear you were a Mexican lawyer. Just don't get too cute with it. We take the constitution as seriously here in the backwaters as they do in the capital. All right, the two of you can go in for an interview with your client, and we'll talk when you're through. By the way, he's already confessed, and there was no coercion involved. I didn't press for too many particulars. I simply asked him whether he did it or not. And if I may make a suggestion, please take a lesson or two in haberdashery before you find yourself in a situation similar to this again. If there's one thing that works against an accused's best interests, it's a sloppy lawyer."

The room didn't have anyone else in it besides Keith. He was sitting alone on a bench, not doing anything. He looked guilty as hell. Not of anything in particular, but just in general. Nonetheless, he had a placid air about him. He was by far the most composed of the three of them. "Okay," said Beef, sitting down next to him. "You need to tell us everything as quickly as you can. I don't know how long they plan to let us talk to you. We told them Vic was your attorney, and now we have to figure out a way of extricating you from this." She looked as if she wanted to throw her arms around him, but was constrained from doing so by Vic's presence. Watching the solicitous, ferociously possessive way she bent over Keith,

Vic could hardly believe he had lain in bed with her the night before, in a long embrace. He felt more than ever like an intruder, a voyeur. Now that he had arrived, and performed the task of gaining for her the entree she had desired, he sensed she wished him gone.

"There's nothing to tell. I killed two men."

"Don't say that," Beef whispered.

"Why not? It's true."

"Were there any witnesses?"

"Nope. We were out in the desert, in the most lonesome place you could imagine."

"That's good," she said. "Tell me about the circumstances. I'm sure there were extenuating circumstances, and I need to know about them if I'm going to get you out of here."

"You oughtn't talk like that, Beef," he said. "Don't forget you're a parole officer. And above all, don't get yourself into a lather. If I feel any regrets, it's on your account, not on theirs."

"I don't care what attitude you take. I'm not going to let them make you stand trial down here. We have no idea how they come to their determinations about innocence or guilt."

"I think I'd be better off if you left me down here. I'm not afraid anymore."

"Please tell me how it happened. Please don't deny me."

"All right," he said. "Not because I'm worried about what they plan to do to me, but just to set the record straight. Because I do have a confession to make--to you, Beef. I did something pretty bad, and I want to be at peace about it. If I'm going to die, or be put away, things have to be set to right, as much as they can be. Let me at least try to explain it. This morning I met up with Charlie, and a sidekick of his, and Gamma Ray. They came down here after Ray and me. I wanted to settle our accounts once and for all. What I didn't tell you—either of you—is that Ray had planned all along to rendezvous with me at the Oasis."

Vic groaned. "You mean that place where I met you?"

"Oh, yeah. It's the most logical place. Right across the state line. It's not that hard to escape from the prison, Beef can vouch for that. And everybody in that place knew about Ray's land deed, though none of us had seen it. Word had it he'd buried a pile of money down here, because he always talked about his underground treasures. Lot of people didn't believe him, thought he was crazy, but some of us did believe, I know I did and I still do. Well, we had agreed that we would rendezvous at the Oasis Casino and Auto Stop on that day. If he got out okay, he was going to bring me down here, give me enough to get me out of hock on my gambling debts. Everything would have been fine, too, because Gamma Ray made it all the way to the casino in Vic's car. Only he changed his mind and gave that deed to Vic, and disappeared.

"Of course, I came along with you all instead, and I was still hoping to get a piece of it. I knew he was headed this way. When we arrived here, and checked into the motel, I was lying awake thinking about it all night while the storm pounded down, and real early, as soon as the rain let up, I set out in the van to go have a look at this Mayan Paradise place.

"But no sooner had I pulled out onto the road than I was flagged down by three men in a white station wagon. It was Gamma Ray, and Charlie was driving, and another fellow along with them was so big he had to ride in back with the seat let down. They'd followed me down, and found him before I did. Ray and I didn't get much of a chance to talk, obviously. Charlie wanted to get straight down to business. He'd been under the impression that Ray himself knew the precise location of the cache, but that night before, he'd led them around to one tract of bare dirt and another, rambling on about this and that like a sage and a kook the way he does. The desert locations all looked pretty much alike, but none of them turned out to be the spot, and apparently it was then, knowing from them that I was down here too, he lied that I had the deed, that he'd given it to me after his escape, had orchestrated with me to meet up with them there, and that I would be able to lead them to it once I arrived. Like a gambler, he was playing a hunch. They were about ready to kill him, I could see that much. But they'd committed themselves that far, and I guess they figured it was worth seeing the business through to the end. And I had copied down the coordinates on the deed, so I knew about where to go.

"I tried to get Charlie to come to a specific agreement with me first about forgiving my debts, but he just kept saying we'd see when we got there. I wasn't in much of a position to argue, and I realized we weren't going to get any more information out of Ray. And they were not in the mood to put up with a lot of bullshit. The only thing I had on my mind was finding that cache and settling up. I hadn't planned on doing them any harm. I got into my van, they in the station wagon, and I started driving south, leading them toward where the tracts of Mayan Paradise were supposed to be located. The terrain was pretty rough.

"But then I got scared. I didn't trust my instincts. Instead, I took a side trail, one of those rutted, impossible ones like the trail we got lost on when Andrea busted the axle on her MG. We drove and we drove, until I was sure there were no people, no animals around, no nothing but land and more land for a long ways. Then I grabbed my cane out of the front seat, and told them we were going to have to do some walking. Some serious walking. I took my Winchester down from its mount, too, and some cartridges out of the glove box. I said that I'd camped out my first night in Bahía, and that there were definitely wild animals prowling about, coyotes or what I wasn't sure, but something had been rustling around near my campsite the whole night long, and I'd heard there were poisonous snakes too. I don't know whether they believed me or not. It's possible the thought made them uneasy. They did keep prodding the reed-grass with sticks as we walked along.

"I suspect, though, that the reason Charlie didn't put up a fuss about me bringing along my rifle is because he knows I'm a coward. I've proved it to him time and again, grovelling, begging for pity. I think as much as anything he enjoyed the idea of me toting that rifle along, because he figured that even if I had a fantasy of using it on them, the mere fact of having a firearm in my hand would make me lose my nerve. Not only make me lose my nerve, but rub in the fact of what a loser I was and the depth of my cowardice. So he said sure, that was no problem. He almost encouraged me to take it. They had guns too, and if anybody had happened along, we probably would have looked to them like a party of hunters down from California for the weekend.

"When we'd walked for a good long time, and them having to keep holding up and wait for me on account of my bad hip, and us not having brought any food or water, and getting thirstier and thirstier, they started grousing, having all their doubts and second thoughts, and accusing Ray of having messed them over, and said one of us for fucking sure better come to this supposed burial spot soon. They were browbeating us, mostly Ray though. Then they actually started beating Ray, hitting him on the shoulders and in the kidneys and in the back of his head with the butts of their guns. I just stood there, watching them fuck him up, watching them maim him to death, while they asked him over and over where's the burial spot motherfucker, where's the burial spot.

"I didn't do anything to stop them. But finally, I heard myself shouting 'Hey!' Both of them stopped beating on Ray, turned to me with angry faces, red and raw as slabs of beef, and I said to them, in a kind of pathetic whisper, 'You've come to the end of the journey and you're standing right on it. This is the burial spot.' Then I raised up my rifle and shot them. First Charlie, then the other fellow. I walked out of there, got in my van, drove here, and told the police what I'd done and where they could find the bodies."

He raised his head and looked at Beef. "I wish I could say I planned it out like that, right from the beginning, and executed my plan down to the last detail. Because I did hate Charlie with a passion. But his death is like everything else in my life. It kind of happened accidentally on purpose. I do feel a little better, though. It's hard to explain, but my mind is a lot easier. The only thing I wish is that I could have done righter by you. Of course I don't expect you to believe me, or to forgive me. I'm not asking for that. Let's just let happen now whatever has to happen."

"We're not giving up," said Vic. "I think we have a decent chance at arguing self-defense. Those men were using coercion against you. They were in the midst of committing one murder, and there's no question that they meant to kill you next." He argued his hypoethetical case with heat, as if he were already in front of a jury, and had been for some time. "You never know beforehand what you'll do under certain extreme circumstances, what you'll be forced to do. You said yourself that it wasn't premeditated. That makes a big difference. It should make a big difference. I haven't passed my bar yet, but I'm a degreed attorney, and I'm almost certain that they'll let me represent you if you have to stand trial. I want to do it. I'm going to start writing down the evidence in your favor as soon as I get back to the motel."

Keith had curled up on the bench, and Beef held his head in her lap. She was stroking his face, and looked up at Vic. "No," she said quietly. "We're not going to do things that way."

"What the hell are you talking about? That's Keith's best chance. His only chance."

"In that case, we'll use your plan as a backup, when there are no alternatives left. There are plenty of other ways of getting at the law. I'm not going to have him stand trial here, among strangers. With our luck, the judge and jury will knock themselves out trying to be fair-minded, and he'll end up rotting down here for the rest of his life. I have an idea I want to try. You just go along with whatever I say, and assume that I'm speaking for both of us when I talk to the captain."

Vic looked around for furniture to kick, but there was none in the room except the bench she and Keith were sitting on. "I'm not going to do anything of the kind. You called me to represent him. Now let me. We have a very good chance of prevailing. The prison break and all that business has no direct bearing on the facts of this case. I think most of it will be disallowed as evidence. This isn't a sham strategy. I really believe myself, in my heart, that Keith acted in self-defense. And that's what you need to defend someone passionately—moral certainty of their innocence." Vic looked to Keith for the barest glimmer of confirmation, but Keith's expression, his closed eyes, yielded nothing. Vic's leg and face had begun to throb almost unbearably. "All right," he said. "I'll go along with your plan, for now."

Keith still said nothing. He stood up and walked to the window to stare out. He didn't turn around when they went out the doorway.

"So," said the captain. "All finished with your informational chat?"

"Yes," said Vic. "Finished for now, anyway."

"In that case, I'd like you to have a look at the bodies." They crossed a courtyard into an annex even smaller than the post. As soon as the door was opened, he could smell the stench of decomposing flesh. The room felt humid, swampy. They hadn't been bothered by insects of any kind during the trip, but swarms of flies buzzed about in the air. It seemed that all the flies in Baja, all two hundred of them or however many there were, had been quarantined in this tiny annex. "I won't keep you here long. I realize it's unpleasant. You can see for yourself that we have no proper place to store the corpses. It's a problem, actually. I could send them up to Ensenada to have them embalmed or cremated, but I don't want to tamper with them until I know the disposition of the case. Needless to say, we don't have a morgue down here. Believe it or not, we don't have much of a need for one. There's not much pollution, still less crime, and even less murder. I can't even remember when the last murder was. Certainly not since I was assigned here, and that was several years ago. Most of the deaths I have to deal with here are those of the tourists who come here, drink too much on their speedboats, misjudge the strength of the Sea of Cortez, and end up drowning." He gave Vic a sardonic glance. "Kayakers supposedly in Baja for scientific purposes, that sort of thing. And in those cases, we simply ship the corpses back to their families. C.O.D., naturally."

Three bodies were laid out on two long tables. Vic's eye lit first on Gamma Ray. Vic wouldn't have mistaken him now, not even remotely, for someone he'd gone to Andover with. He was stripped bare. Every hardship he'd ever suffered, every nick and scar, was visible on his head and body. Despite the fact that his mouth remained open, drawn preternaturally apart into an oracular O, he didn't look very prophetic. So many contusions covered his face it was difficult to separate out one from the next. Beside him, on the same table, lay the corpse of a man he could only suppose to be Charlie. A blanket was drawn up discreetly above his waist, probably to cover the place where the bullet had entered his body. There wasn't anything terribly special about him except for the fact that he was dead. His hair was lank, with a balding patch on one side, and he had freckles.

A body of girth, massive even in death, took up the entirety of the other table, the feet even hanging off at the end. Even though most of his face was gone, Vic recognized him at once. He was still wearing the sleeveless vest with metal studs on the pocket, and it still reached only halfway around his beer belly. The severely barbered haircut, or what was left of it, hadn't grown out much since he'd last seen him, a couple of days before. The only thing Vic could think of, the only thing that preyed upon his mind while he gazed upon that gigantic corpse, was that the biker would never get to finish his course in Hotel and Motel Management.

They stepped back outside, and the captain closed the door of the makeshift morgue behind him. "The question before us is what to do about the detainee. As you can see, I'm not in a position to delay the matter for very long. Last night we had to keep chasing wild animals away from the building. There are only three of us at this post. We don't have the manpower for that sort of thing, between reports of theft, car trouble, people drowning, lost passports. The tourists who pass through here have caused me nothing but headaches and troubles. They must think we have no problems of our own, and exist for the sole purpose of adjudicating their difficulties."

"We're as anxious to resolve this matter as you are," said Vic.

"That may be so," said the captain. "But I must forewarn you that if you're about to proclaim the innocence of your client, or tell me that he acted in self-defense, then this case will probably drag on for quite a while. It's true that there were no witnesses, but his voluntary confession complicates matters. The way these things work, the inquest could go on for weeks, and possibly even months. To tell you the truth, I wish to God he'd never come in here and confessed. In that desolate stretch where the bodies fell, it might have taken weeks before anyone turned them up, and the suspect would have been long gone by then, I presume. And the carrion birds doubtless would have carried off the evidence as well. Frankly, I'd love nothing more than to wash my hands of this whole troublesome affair, but unfortunately, those same hands are tied by the Mexican constitution. I don't see any way out but to proceed."

The captain obviously didn't care one way or the other about the alleged crime. The death of the three men didn't cause him any more consternation than he might have felt on watching Lucas thoughtlessly throw a Seven-Up can into the sea, or coming upon a hunter from California who had exceeded his game limit. Inadvertently or on purpose, a large infraction or a minor one—it was all the same to him. Like a weary game warden who knows he can't stop the onslaught of poachers and litterbugs, he looked prepared to devote whatever portion of his life was necessary to seeing the matter through to its conclusion.

"We have no plans of proclaiming his innocence," Beef said. "Quite the contrary."

"*Mande?*" said the captain. He couldn't seem to believe his ears. Vic was having trouble with his hearing as well. Had the captain suddenly switched into Spanish, or had the three of them been speaking Spanish all along? He felt obliged to translate Beef's remark for the captain's benefit. "*Ella dice que no queremos mantener su inocencia de ninguna manera.*"

"Oh?"

"That's right." Beef was now speaking English, forcing Vic to continue translating her comments to the captain. "I'm personally convinced that he deliberately tracked down both of these men and shot them in cold blood."

Los cazó y los mató a sangre fría. "And murder is only one of this man's worries. Keith Jackson is wanted by the U.S. government for all kinds of misdeeds. He was an accomplice in the escape of one of the dead men in the other room there this past week, one we've been trying to recapture. They, along with the other two men, were involved in illegal gambling, extortion, auto theft. The station wagon outside was stolen, and used to transport the prisoner across the U.S. border. It's a very sticky case, and one we're trying to resolve as quietly as possible—within the limits the law allows, of course." *Es un asunto muy delicado, y lo queremos resolver lo más suavemente que sea posible—dentro de lo que la ley permitiera, por supuesto.* He was trying to be as literal and affectless as possible, but he felt that his tone and syntax lent each sentence, each phrase, a subtle, sinister, unctuous tone of complicity, of a deal being cut.

Beef handed the captain the documents she'd been carrying with her in a worn leather pouch. "These are statements to that effect, signed by the warden of the penitentiary. If you don't read English, the attorney of the accused can translate them for you."

"I can read them just fine," said the captain. "One nice thing about legal documents—they're equally unintelligible in all languages. I always feel like I'm attending high Latin Mass when I have one before me. Hmm. We did receive a bulletin about that station wagon outside, but the rest of this is news to me."

"I'm sure you're familiar with the extradition treaty recently signed between our two governments. I know there's been a lot of friction between the two countries, but this seemed to be one thing they could agree on in good faith. The treaty allows for the immediate extradition of known criminals who have committed grave federal offenses, and who are considered especially dangerous by the state. The treaty is meant to expedite necessary extraditions without undue bureaucractic interference. We want to prosecute and punish Keith Jackson to the full extent our laws permit, and I'm afraid that if he's tried here in Mexico, he might get off with only manslaughter, or might be let off altogether."

"I see," said the captain, poring over the documents one by one. The expression of stern tension on his face began to give way to a look of relief. As he worked his way through the documents, he began to smile, and chuckle softly, as if he were reading a letter from a very old and dear friend who had asked him to receive the bearer of the letter with courtesy. "Well, it all looks very clear cut to me. Your papers are all in order. The only thing I can do is commend the entire case over into your hands as the designated representative of the U.S. penal system. It's completely out of my power now." He almost seemed ready to burst into peals of laughter. "The law speaks with absolute clarity in this instance, and there's absolutely nothing I can do to gainsay it."

Beef struggled to contain herself. "You mean you're giving him to us?"

"Yes, I am. I'm sure you'll mete out justice as you see fit. If I can make another recommendation—I don't know what direction you're going to be heading in, but I'd get going as soon as I could. If you dawdle too long about leaving, a raft of underemployed and overzealous attorneys from Mexico City might get wind of this, and next thing you know they'll be swarming around here like flies, studying the subclauses of the extradition treaty for loopholes. But, I'm only obliged to enforce the law as it stands at present. If they want to change the laws, that's up to them."

"Thank you," said Beef. "Thank you for being so understanding."

"I'm only as understanding as I need to be. By the way, there is one other little thing. Since you'll be needing all the evidence you can muster to prosecute this case efficiently, to the full extent of the law, as you say, I'm sure you won't mind taking all three of those corpses off my hands." He smiled the beneficent smile of a public servant. "They're certainly not doing me any good. I'll make sure you have all the official letters necessary to get you to the border without any misunderstandings. How you deal with your own customs officials is your problem. I've heard they're not quite so flexible as ours when it comes to importing dead people, unless the dead people happen to be ancient Mayans and Aztecs. Of course, there are an awful lot of desolate open stretches of country between here and Ensenada in case you need to, you know, bury some garbage or anything. Just don't leave it above ground. We don't like litterbugs."

There was a long moment of silence. Beef, almost swooning with the realization that Keith had been released, hardly seemed to hear what the captain was saying.

"Of course," said Vic. "Yes, we'll be happy to dispose of the bodies— that is, to have them at our disposal."

"I thought you might want them."

Vic knew they ought to take the captain's advice and get moving as quickly as possible, before he had a chance to rethink his position. All the same, he loitered.

The captain had already sat down at one of the typewriters to begin typing the necessary letters. "Is there something else?" he asked without looking up, a hint of impatience in his voice.

"One minor request," said Vic. "I was wondering if it might not also make sense for us take along the station wagon parked outside. It's a crucial part of the evidence, since it was used as part of the alleged escape. That's the pursuit that brought us down here in the first place. And also, if we're going to be hauling three corpses along with us, we're going to need some way to transport them. All we have is the van we came in."

The captain's two index fingers flew over the keys of the typewriter with all deliberate speed. He gave a gruff, irascible grunt. "I'm afraid that won't be possible." He stopped typing and gave Vic a hard, imperious look. "If you plan to use the car as evidence concerning your client, someone will have to be sent down later to retrieve it. There's a lien on it. As I said, we received a bulletin about that station wagon on our telex a couple of days ago."

"Concerning the prison break, you mean?"

"Oh, no. Nothing to do with that. I never heard a word about a prison break until the two of you showed up. We're always gettting police bulletins about automobiles registered in California, because when cars get stolen, the thieves sometimes change the plates on them and bring them down here to chop shops. Spare parts are at a premium in Baja. The police up there in the U.S. ask us to keep an eye out, as part of a reciprocal law enforcement accord we have going. Anyway, that station wagon is registered in the name of a person named—Andrea Simmons, Simpson—something like that. I can't remember the exact name. Those Anglo surnames all sound alike to me. Not only has the California registration on the station wagon expired, but it seems this Simons owes a couple of thousand dollars in parking fines of one kind and another on that vehicle. I can't release the vehicle, murder or no murder, until those fines have been cleared, and it has a valid registration sticker on it. Some things we can bend the rules on. Other things we can't. You'll just have to keep the windows open on your van, and hope the rain keeps the weather cool for a couple of days. Or figure out some other solution. One of you needs to sign this release form. It doesn't matter which. I just need a John Hancock. Isn't that how you say it up there—John Hancock? Who is he, anyway?"

That night, at dusk, Vic, Beef, and Keith retrieved the three corpses wrapped in blankets and plastic sheets, as they'd agreed to do, and put them into the sleeping bags, still damp from the storm. They drove outside Bahía, heading westward, until they reached a stretch of plain below some foothills that looked to be made more of earth than rock. They rattled along with all the windows down, and several times Keith had to pull over so that one or the other of them could throw up.

They had passed through a number of canebrakes, or what looked in the headlights to be canebrakes, which made Vic believe that the earth in that stretch of valley was arable, and might be comparatively soft. The stench had become overpowering and they couldn't afford the luxury of looking around much longer. Beef had bought a galvanized shovel and a lantern from a farm supply store at a ridiculously inflated price. Walking across a field in the darkness with her to test its soil, Vic felt a bit of spring beneath his shoes. "This will have to do," he said.

Keith held the lantern while Vic and Beef took turns digging. The recent rain had made the first few inches of topsoil loamier than it might have been otherwise, but the dirt nonetheless came loose in slivers and clumps, and they had to jump on the shovel with both feet to carve out even a small space. Vic's original plan had been to dig separate graves for each of the three men, and try to put them down far enough that they wouldn't be dug up, or have the concavities in which they lay precipitously exposed by another burst of inclement weather, a flash flood, the erosions of wind. Unless their bones were carried off by foraging animals, and unless any major global climatic changes took place in the foreseeable future, the aridity of the desert and the sulfites in the soil might preserve the skeletons intact for centuries, maybe millenia. Vic dug with intensity, slicing off cakes of packed, parched earth until the sockets in his shoulders burned, until his clothes were soaked in sweat. He could feel blisters forming on his hands. His body trembled with the effort. He had to remove his shirt, and steam evanesced from his skin into the chill night.

"It's no use," Beef said irritably. "We need to get out of here. I don't know why you insist on separate spaces. It would take us all of tonight and all of tomorrow to make the kind of graves you have in mind. Let's just put the three of them in one grave. We can't place any markers here anyway. The thing we want is for no one to unearth them for a few weeks. After that, it doesn't matter."

"Shut up. I'm not asking anybody else to dig. You can go back and sit in the van until I'm through if you want." Clammy, knee deep in the ditch, his nose running, he dug, and dug, and dug some more. He savaged the dirt with the tip of the shovel, bending the tip when he struck patches of rock. His strokes became sloppy. In the end, they had to bury the corpses in the most efficient way, as she had suggested.

Even though Andrea remained weak, the doctor confirmed that the spontaneous abortion hadn't endangered her life. Unlike Vic, she'd had a good night's sleep, and looked well on her way to recovery from the immediate episode.

She'd certainly bounced back, said the doctor, she was lucky to be so young, but what she needed now was prolonged rest, whether here or somewhere else it didn't matter, and someone to look after her for a while. No drastic intervention was required, but rather, simple attention to her daily needs until she regained her strength. Vic waited in a hard plastic seat on the other side of the consultation curtain. Did she have someone who could do that for her? "Yes," he heard her answer automatically, dispassionately, wearily, as if assenting to rote instructions for penance in a confessional. Was there someone who could make sure she got to wherever it was she planned to go? Yes. Did she know where she was going to go? No, she didn't. Had the young man sitting outside come to escort her back to her lodgings? Yes, he had. The doctor hoped so, because she wasn't in any kind of condition to be striking out on her own. She'd been through an ordeal, when all was said and done. All right then, he wished her well, but he couldn't help also observing that the young man didn't appear to be in much better shape than her. It was going to be the blind leading the blind, from the looks of it.

When the two of them had walked outside, Vic let Andrea know what had happened. He said that Keith had been charged with murder but released from custody. The news of the deaths didn't shock her as much as he thought it might. "I told Keith we would take a short excursion out to Mayan Paradise. Keith still insists on seeing the site. Beef wants to get out of the country as quickly as possible. But when she saw Keith perk up a little when I mentioned visiting Mayan Paradise, she agreed to go along. Keith knows the way, more or less. He has an idea something valuable is buried there. I don't think he'll find anything, but maybe it will take his mind off these past couple of days. Maybe it will take all our minds off things. If you want, though, I can drop you at the motel, and we'll probably be back within half a day."

"You want to see it too, don't you?"

"I thought I'd tag along."

"No, I mean apart from Keith. Something's still drawing you there."

"Yes. "

"Well, this is the last leg of the trip. I might as well go with you. I've come this far." She allowed herself one brief, small smile. "I didn't make it to Manhattan."

"What about the doctor's orders?"

"What about them? It seems I've been released into your custody." They touched hands briefly. Seated in the van, he jiggled the ignition switch to try to make it turn over. Her face was to the window, but he could tell that she was crying. If she noticed the peculiar smell in the van, it didn't seem to concern her, or to fall outside the range of her expectation.

"I'm sorry, Andrea. I'm sorry for everything."

"Don't apologize. It's me. I just feel completely empty. When I first found out I was pregnant, and had made up my mind to have the abortion, the idea really didn't bother me that much. I wanted to do it alone. What bothered me was the thought of you going along with me, of my having to sit through a lecture by some avuncular, well-meaning gynecologist, and then to come out and have you waiting for me in the lobby, trying to make me feel that everything was going to be all right. I would have done any-thing to avoid going through that. I didn't want to make myself vulnerable again in that way. And now, here I am, sitting in the front seat, having listened to the doctor's lecture and walked out of the clinic with you."

During the drive to Mayan Paradise, she sat motionless. Watching the landscape roll by, he was struck by the unrelenting sameness of its tortuous topography. The first time he'd passed through, it had appeared so spectacular, so vital, that he thought he could never imagine growing tired of it or taking it for granted, not in a million years. Each morning, as he awoke in his cottage and stepped out onto the beach, the frothy whitecaps on one side, and the sharply defined buttes on the other, would electrify him. Now, the landscape held no more interest for him than the stretches of industrial wasteland in New Jersey might possess for a longtime commuter into Manhattan.

They passed road markers now and then that said *Vado.* Vic seemed to remember the word referred to the ford in a stream, but although the road dipped, there was no water present alongside it, not even in the wake of the storm. They had gone gradually inland from the coast, and the sea was no longer visible. The clouds had dissipated, leaving nothing but open sky. Coming upon the sign for their turnoff, they almost missed it. In fact, they had driven past it, and only then did Keith notice the weatherbeaten placard, which had been facing the other way, in his rearview mirror. Mayan Paradise 3 km. *Modelos De Lujo.* An arrow pointed eastward. Keith eased the van along the pocked pathway. The odor ingrained in the van had begun to subside, or rather was beginning to be replaced, overpowered by another stench, a chemical sweetness, a perfume pervading the air.

When they pulled into the site, vast tracts of razed earth spread out before them, more parched and naked even than the desert floor he'd grown accustomed to seeing. The place looked like an abandoned archeological excavation. Deep trenches had been cut throughout the length and breadth of the tracts. A few bulldozers and backhoes were parked here and there, unmanned and unattended to. Dozens of crumbling pyramids of dirt, equidistant from one another, hulked like a skyline of burial mounds. One bulldozer moved among the mounds, solitary and ostentatious in its noise and its shroud of blue smoke. Its claw bit into one of the mounds, lurched and swiveled, and dropped its crusty mass into a trench.

Vic asked Keith whether he wanted to get out and look around, but Keith said he was too tired. Still, Vic could see him trembling with expectation. He was like a person who receives an important letter and asks someone else to open it. Or, more accurately, a desperate person who has spent his last dollar on a lottery ticket and sends someone else into the convenience store to buy the newspaper where the winning numbers have been published.

Beef and Andrea made no motion of stirring either, so Vic got out alone and walked toward the bulldozer, trying to ignore the pain in his leg, navigating between two raw trenches, taking long strides, like someone who distrusts the surveyor's fictive grids, and has to take the actual measure of his parcel of land for himself. He didn't seem to be coming any closer to the bulldozer. The parallel lines made by the trenches appeared to converge in the distance, where he knew the Sea of Cortez lay, out of his sight and beyond the visible horizon. If he scaled one of the promontories made by the mounds, he would be able to see it. But he knew that if the trenches were truly parallel, in pure mathematical exactitude, that he would never reach the apparent vanishing point.

Coming within the funnel of noise that enveloped the man wearing earmuffs, housed inside the bulldozer's protective booth, Vic began to wave, trying to attract his attention. The ground shook beneath his feet in a continuous tremor. Glyphs incised in the treads of the oversized tires zig-zagged skyward. At last the bulldozer operator shut off the machinery, climbed out of his booth, and dropped to the ground. He wore workpants, a checkered shirt, and a brittle straw cowboy hat over his earmuffs. Even on the ground, the man continued to create the optical illusion of being taller than Vic. He had to be at least six feet if he was an inch. Perhaps he really was over six feet. He had a goatee and his eyes were seamed with intricate patterns of wrinkles, ones that crisscrossed without any semblance of symmetry.

"Is this Mayan Paradise?" Vic asked the man.

The man nodded and lifted his straw hat with one hand so he could take off his earmuffs. "You don't have to shout. I can hear you. Yeah, it was going to be. What's your concern in it?"

"I have a deed to one of the plots."

"I'm afraid you're a little late. Didn't you get your letter?"

"What letter?"

"The development group sent out letters to all the people who bought plots down here, telling them they had so many weeks to cash in for their RealBuks. Funny you didn't get yours."

"Oh. Well, somebody else gave me this deed. I sort of came by it secondhand, and wanted to see what the place looked like."

"You're looking at it. It was going to be gorgeous. Not as big as Cancun, but a lot nicer. More exclusive. Landscaped. They were even talking about devising an irrigation system so they could put in a golf course. The developers had the whole thing mapped out, obtained all their licenses, surveyed, and were ready to start digging foundations. But then this tract of land got caught up in a dispute between the U.S. and Mexican governments."

"What kind of dispute?"

"I don't know the ins and outs of it. I mostly just hear what gets passed around the workplace. Us locals were all hoping this project would keep us employed for a couple of years anyway. There's not much work to be had down here. But there was some kind of international tariff thing, and the Mexican government retaliated by threatening to nationalize some of the interests that they'd assigned to the U.S. They didn't really go through with it the way they threatened, but they did pick out a few projects to make examples of. This was one of them. They hold the subsoil rights to the Mayan Paradise development, and right in the middle of this dispute, somebody—not even an archeologist, just some treasure hunter or other—found a couple of clay pots in this area. The Mexican government used the find as a pretext for saying they had to stop the development in its tracks, so they could bring in a team of archeologists to explore."

He shook his head and laughed. "And, of course, they did it in the style they've done everything else in this misbegotten country. The developers tried to call their bluff. Said if there was really something down there, they ought to go ahead and see what it was, and not string it out over the next decade, a shovelful at a time. There were accusations, and counteraccusations, and finally our government just came in here, hell-bent, with tons of heavy machinery, and started tearing the ground apart, like they were strip-mining iron ore instead of looking for precious artifacts. They finished digging in three days, nonstop. Dirt flying every which way. I don't think they expected to find anything. It was more like vengeance. They wanted to tear the place up as badly as they could. But it turns out there was all kinds of priceless stuff down there. Vessels, figurines. Who would have thought? It must have been some kind of religious spot, sacred.

It's amazing nobody had come across it before, it being such a large cache. Of course, the way they tore up the ground, they completely destroyed about ninety per cent of the goods. Nothing much left but pottery fragments. Now they'll spend the next hundred years trying to put them back together. That's the PRI for you. Do you feel all right? You're looking a little woozy. I have a thermos of coffee up in my bulldozer if you want some."

"No, I'm okay. I think I'll sit down here on the ground for a minute. What do they plan to do with the site now?"

"As you can imagine, crushing that archeological find just made them madder than before. So they told the developers they were going to continue to exercise their subsoil rights, right down to the letter of the law. Now they're trucking in toxic chemical waste from some of the plants and refineries further up on the peninsula. They're going to turn this tract of land into the nastiest sinkhole outside Mexico City. As if to say, okay, we've used our part, now you can go right ahead and build whatever you like on top of it. I'm in the middle of covering up one of the trenches where they've stored some concrete blocks they unloaded last week. It's kind of a shame. I don't know what's in them, and I don't want to know. I suppose I ought to be wearing a face mask. But after a while, you don't notice the smell so much, when you're surrounded by it all the time. I expect in another ten years we'll all be about ten feet tall around here. That's the PRI's answer to malnutrition. If I was you, I'd go cash that deed in quick as I could. Last I heard, that development company was getting ready to file for bankruptcy."

The heaviness in Vic's legs as he walked was so great that he had to keep stopping to rest. It seemed a long way back. He thought he'd been tired all along, but now, a weariness settled over him the like of which he'd never known before. The bulldozer had started up again behind him. The trench to his left was wonderfully deep, infallibly deep. No one could fault him for giving in to fatigue. Even the universe was getting a little tired. There was the van, however, coming toward him like some annoying, woolly, prehistoric beast, some aberrant survival, almost unrecognizable beneath its patina of road grit.

"You looked like you were kind of weaving," said Keith, getting out and taking hold of him. Vic felt as though he were being hoisted up by a much stronger, much healthier person. He kept forgetting how solid Keith's grip was. "I noticed you weren't walking a very straight line." He looked into Vic's eyes. "I'm doing a whole lot better today. How about you?"

"You were right," said Vic. "There was an enormous archeological find, some time ago, weeks or months, I'm not sure. It's all been smashed to pieces. I don't remember reading about it."

He heard an expulsion of breath, as though Keith had been hit in the stomach. But then, Keith drew another breath. "Well, that's too bad. My inventory's kind of low all around, and I was hoping to replenish it." He squinted thoughtfully. "But I'll have to see what else I can scare up. When we passed through a little settlement north of Bahía I noticed a whole mess of plaster birdbaths. They were kind of unique, almost like sculptures, nice detail work, and each one different from the others. Looked like whoever made them used quality materials, too. I might just have to load up with some of those, if I can get them for the right price, and see what I can do with them."

Vic smiled. "They sound nice. They sound really nice."

"Keith and I are leaving today," Beef said on the drive back to the motel, in an offhand tone of voice that she had probably been practicing all morning.

"Where are you going?"

"We're not sure. We thought we might spend a few weeks in Belize, as long as our money holds out, or we can make some more somewhere. We'll ferry our van across the Sea of Cortez, and travel down the mainland from there. I've always wanted to spend some time in Belize. The snorkeling there is supposed to be some of the best in the world."

"Yes, I've heard that too."

"I have to write up a summary of Gamma Ray's case, and send it back, to close out the file for good. I'm sure the warden will be very satisfied at how the matter was resolved without causing anybody any trouble or suffering. And then there's my resignation too, of course. In writing. I have some severance pay and vacation days coming to me, so I don't want to drop out of sight completely until I get at least that. Maybe I'll have them send my check to the American Express office in Mexico City. I have a feeling we're going to need it."

She turned to Andrea. "I don't mean to cut the two of you out. You're welcome to come along with us for a while, if you want. I just didn't know what plans you had."

Vic gave Andrea a questioning look, a look as blank as a palimpsest, a look into which, or out of which, she probably could have read anything she wanted. She shook her head. "We can drop you at the bus station," said Beef. "If you're short of cash, I can spring for a couple of tickets. I'm sorry about your not being able to recover the station wagon. And I guess you'll have to come back to get your MG." She held a plastic bag filled with unbroken sea shells. "I'd appreciate it if you dropped these by my neighbor Francisco's house, if you're ever in that area again."

"I'll make a point of being there," said Vic, taking them from her out-stretched hand. "I'll keep them with me until then. Do you want to go back to San Diego?" he asked, turning to Andrea.

"Yes. For a few days anyway, to see a doctor and to try to get my personal affairs in order. Insofar as that's possible."

"Since I'm the most disorderly part of your personal affairs, and since you're going to be trying to straighten them out anyway, would you mind if I came along with you?"

"I think that would be all right. Yes, I think I would like that a lot."

Even with the Sea of Cortez so near, barely out of sight, the breeze had slackened to almost nothing. The air was full of a neutral stillness. It wasn't hot yet, but the lack of even a single wisp of cloud on the horizon or in the sky meant that it was going to turn hot again soon, hot as it had been all summer, hot as the insufferable night Vic had spent closed up tight in the back of the station wagon, parked in the marina on the shore of the Great Salt Lake. It might turn so hot, and it might be so long until the next rain, that the Sea of Cortez would keep on shrinking, the level growing lower and lower until its water was as distilled, salty, and solid-seeming as the Great Salt Lake itself.

The redeye was loaded with passengers and looked ready to depart, but for some unexplained reason the bus remained in its bay. The driver sat in his high-backed chair, scribbling on a ledger with a pencil stub, studiously ignoring occasional halfhearted calls from the back to get underway. Mostly, though, the passengers around Vic sat in patient silence, reading newspapers or soap opera comic books, staring absently at their reflections in the darkened glass, or rearranging cloth bundles as shapeless as fattened hens nesting in the overhead racks. The bus from Bahía to Ensenada only ran twice a week, the ticketseller had said. So there was nothing to do now besides wait for whatever unforeseen kink had arisen to work itself out.

Every seat was occupied. Vic wondered where all the passengers had come from. He had no idea there could be this many people around in Bahía de los Angeles who had business requiring them to travel overland for most of the night. The majority of them, though quiet, seemed wakeful, excited, as though about to embark on a spectacular journey, rather than a bumpy ride through the darkness to a noisy, smelly town up the peninsula. He supposed that the trip in itself, regardless of its object, had a way of evoking that emotion in people. He felt a sense of restless anticipation within himself, too.

The two men in the seat in front of him, who for Vic existed only as a pair of moving straw hats and voices to go with them, were having an animated conversation about the best way to gauge rainfall accurately. One said all you had to do was set a jar outdoors, and see how much was in it when the rain stopped. The other one claimed that no, you had to be more scientific about it. Different amounts fell in different places, even over a small area, so you had to spread your collectors around the countryside, and average them out. Only then could you even begin to think you had formed the roughest picture of what had happened during the night. The problem was, he'd been meaning to test his hypothesis out, but had slept right through the storm. It hadn't even woken him up, and he didn't know anything about its having stormed at all until he went outdoors the next morning and saw that a whole section of his fence had been blown down. He spoke cheerfully, as if recounting a piece of unexpected good fortune that had befallen him. Both of them lamented the fact that there was no way of telling when they might have another chance to prove which of their theories came closest to the truth. The first man, by way of offering condolences, asked the second if he would like a cigarette.

Across the aisle, a little girl in shorts stood in her window seat, languidly surveying the contents of the bus as she crunched on a stalk of cane. Her grandmother, or whoever the woman sitting next to her was, wore a black shawl over her head, and kept herself busy doing embroidery.

She was elderly, with a no-nonsense expression. The old woman kept her charge in check without having to look over at her. The little girl had calibrated precisely the boundaries of her freedom, the limits of her chaperone's tolerance, and all of this was apparent at a glance to the most casual observer. But the girl didn't seem troubled overmuch by the arrangement. She squatted down to get a closer look at her grandmother's stitchery, breathing in her ear. "*Déjame*," said the woman impatiently. The girl snuggled closer, crunching her stalk of cane.

Andrea shifted in her window seat, trying in vain to find a more comfortable position. She had fallen asleep already, almost as soon as they'd taken their seats, the right side of her face squashed against the glass. The sweater she'd been using to cushion her cheek had fallen to the seat, and Vic tried to replace the sweater as best he could without waking her. The automatic front door of the bus hissed shut, and the engine began to rumble. The occupants seemed on the verge of making collective progress, and fell momentarily, hopefully silent, but the driver wasn't making any promises. He opened the folding door again, by hand, and stepped outside to attend to some last-minute detail. There was the creak of the luggage compartment below being opened, and cavernous rummaging in the bowels. Vic produced an apple from his knapsack, a pocketknife from his pocket, and began to peel. Half an inch or so of fruit flesh came off with the peel as he worked around the apple in small slices. "Give that here," he heard a stern and peremptory voice beside him command. When he looked across the aisle, the woman in the black shawl was holding her hand out. "You're mauling it," she said. "I can't bear to watch somebody ruin a perfectly good apple like that."

He gave her the apple and the knife. She peeled with a clean spiraling motion, and the skin fell away in a single uninterrupted piece, without any flesh clinging to it. The hard-used knife that Keith had given him just before they parted company suddenly seemed razor sharp, and the peeling of the apple the simplest of tasks. "You see how it's done?" the woman asked, holding the pared piece of fruit up for his inspection. The flesh shone white, unbruised, and its shape was satisfactorily round and smooth, except for the places he'd gouged at the top, which looked as though someone had already taken intemperate bites out of them. "There." The woman wiped the pocketknife clean on her shawl, snapped it shut, and handed both it and the apple back to him. "It's the easiest thing in the world if you'll only concentrate." He began to eat, welling up with a mixture of gratitude and embarrassment.

The driver was mounted in his seat again, and the interior lights went off. The bus lurched, accelerated, and in a surprisingly short time the street lamps of the town had disappeared, and the passengers were hurtling and shaking together through blank, dark space. There was a final, general shifting and settling as they accommodated themselves to their places as best they could. Andrea's sleeping outline was jarred whenever they hit a bump, but she didn't stir. Vic bent over and kissed her neck. The motion of the bus was starting to make him drowsy too. He turned and peered down the length of the aisle, trying to remember exactly where he had crammed his jacket in the overhead rack opposite. A pillow, even a makeshift one, would be a comfort, but he couldn't make out anything, and at last he gave up and hunkered down in his seat. Well, it didn't matter. The insomnia that had been plaguing him all these weeks had passed in some undefined but definitive way, he could sense that it had, and tonight, in the most unlikely of places, the redeye express, he would sleep soundly and long, no matter what the inconveniences or reasons to stay up gnashing his teeth. He was going to sleep the sleep of the just, whether he deserved to or not. Vic felt himself slipping off, and didn't try to stop the fall. That apple had hit the spot. He was beginning to feel almost human.

Baja is Johnny Payne's third novel. His writing has appeared in *Southern Review*, *Triquarterly*, and numerous other quarterlies and literary journals. In addition to fiction, he has written several nonfiction books, plus two musical plays, *The Devil in Disputanta* (produced by Loyala University, Chicago, in 1996) and an historical drama of colonial Peru, *The Serpent's Lover*. Presently at work on a fourth novel, *Dope*, he lives with his wife, Miriam, and their two children in Boca Raton, Florida, where he teaches fiction writing at Florida-Atlantic University.